kilTer

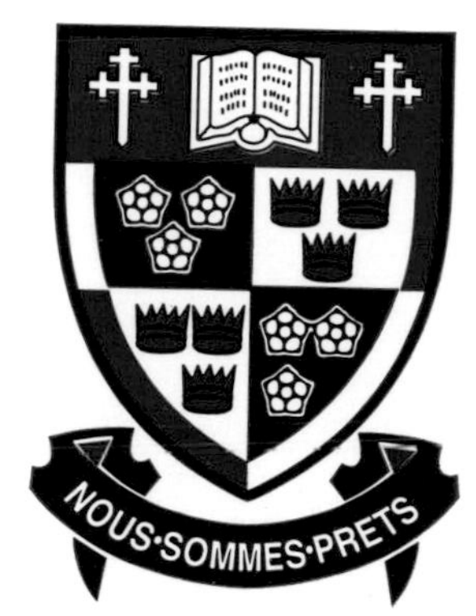
NOUS·SOMMES·PRETS
SIMON FRASER UNIVERSITY
W.A.C. BENNETT LIBRARY

kilTer:
55 fictions

jOhn gouLd

TURNSTONE PRESS

Turnstone Press
607-100 Arthur Street
Artspace Building
Winnipeg, MB
R3B 1H3 Canada
www.TurnstonePress.com

Turnstone Press gratefully acknowledges the assistance of The Canada Council for the Arts, the Manitoba Arts Council, the Government of Canada through the Book Publishing Industry Development Program and the Government of Manitoba through the Department of Culture, Heritage and Tourism, Arts Branch, for our publishing activities.

Cover design: Tétro Design
Interior design: Sharon Caseburg
Printed and bound in Canada by Friesens for Turnstone Press.

National Library of Canada Cataloguing in Publication Data

Gould, John, 1959-
Kilter : 55 fictions / John Gould.

ISBN 0-88801-280-2

I. Title.
PS8563.O8446K44 2003 C813'.54 C2003-910340-4
PR9199.3.G653K44 2003

Turnstone Press is committed to reducing the consumption of old growth forests in the books we publish. This book is printed on acid-free paper that is 100% ancient forest free.

For Sandy

cOntents

kilTer

two things toGether

I liked it better back when my son was into stuff I could understand. Sex, drugs, rock 'n' roll. Or rap, I guess you'd call it, *Yo, mofo*, kind of thing, the white boy's black dream. The big challenge in those days was to keep myself upright on the couch late enough at night to catch him creeping in, reeking of rum and Pepsi and Players Light, mauve hair all mussed up, buttons in all the wrong button holes. What would his mother have said? I'd ask myself.

"What would your mother have said?" I'd ask him.

We'd embrace, stagger off to our separate bedrooms and collapse on top of the covers. As far as my career as a single parent has gone it was pretty much the high point.

But he's seventeen now, that's ancient history.

Take tonight. I offered him a crisp twenty and the car keys. I offered to clear out if he and a girl needed a little quality time.

"It's okay, Dad," he told me. "I'm just going to take it easy."

And don't I know what *that* means.

About an hour ago I found I couldn't stand it any more. I muted the tube—"Xena, Warrior Princess" suddenly falling silent—and pussyfooted down the hall to his bedroom. I cocked my head at his door, not a sound. I gave it a gentle tap. Still nothing. I turned the knob, slunk on in there.

It took my eyes several moments to adjust to the room's dim, incense-laced light. There were stacks of books all over the damn place, wonky highrises. There were candles in rows on the floor—they might have been landing lights spied through the smog at LAX. In the position of control tower sat my son. He was sweat-panted, bare-chested. His legs were pretzeled up under him, his hands laced at his belly as though he were offering somebody a boost.

"'S'up?" I said in the ghetto-speak he favoured not so long ago.

My son's eyes opened, eventually, and he peered up at me. He seemed puzzled, seemed to be trying to place me. It was the same look his mother used to give me when I'd bend over her bed, right at the end there. And the same eyes—heavy-lidded, and what they call hazel.

After a long silence my son spoke one word. "*Anahata*."

"How's that?" I squatted down beside him—just a couple of cowpokes staring into a fire.

"Dad, do you really—"

"Yip." You have to get them talking, this much I know.

My son sighed. "*Anahata*," he said again. "The heart centre. A twelve-petaled lotus, on each petal a letter—" and he made a bunch of noises, rapid-fire, like our cat Cooper chittering at a sparrow he can't quite reach. "Its sound is the *Anahata Sabda*," he went on, as best I could make out. "That's the sound that comes without the striking of any two things together, Dad. Within it there's a blue six-sided star, and the divine—" somebody or other. "She's four-armed, she holds a noose and a skull. She makes the sign of blessing and the sign that dispels fear."

Finally, a word I recognized. "Fear?" I said. "What are you afraid of?"

"Same thing everybody's afraid of. I'm afraid of everything."

"Oh, right," I said. "So, you're, what . . . picturing all this stuff in your head somehow?"

"I'm seeing it," he said. "I'm seeing the seven centres, one after another, from the base of my spine up to the crown of my head. I'm raising the goddess up to be reunited with the god, female with male, form with formlessness. Finite with infinite."

"Fine," I said. "But I mean . . . why?"

He grimaced—give me strength. "*Laya*," he said. "Dissolution, Dad. Undoing the world."

At this point our chat just seemed to, I don't know, fizzle. I couldn't think of anything else to ask him, so I asked him if he wanted a sandwich.

"No thanks, Dad."

"A pop?"

"No thanks."

So I left him to it. I padded back out here, poured myself a couple more fingers of the smoky single malt I splurged on the other day—I've sworn off special occasions, I just nip from it at random. I left the tube turned down—Xena had given way to news, survivors picking through a bombed-out building—and since then I've been sitting here, pondering things by its flickering light.

Why is the light from a television set always blue? This is one of the things I've been pondering. No matter what colours are up there on the screen, the light flooding your room is blue. Why? I don't get it. I don't get a lot of things, more all the time if I'm not mistaken. An infinite number of things, probably, though to tell the truth infinity is one more subject on which I'm a trifle weak. Every once in a while I sip my Scotch, feel it burning its way down, down to the heart of me. That's another thing. Heart?

leathEr

T

Jan picks up the framed photo of herself from her brother's desk. Five years out of date, it must be—her hair almost to her waist, the back of what's-his-name's red, rust-pocked Volvo visible behind her. Henry's Volvo. And she looks so *happy*.

Did Lance notice her there often, she wonders, during the course of his day? Did he wink at her between patients, consult her when he happened upon a symptom especially puzzling to him, especially disturbing? Or did he finally just stop seeing her, as he must have stopped seeing that Leaning Tower of Pisa paperweight, for instance—a memento from one of their parents' trips, no doubt, a conciliatory nod to his craving for kitsch—or that Liza Minelli letter opener?

Jan sets the photo back in its place, precisely, as the police have insisted she do. No way to be sure what's evidence and what isn't.

The evidence Jan herself seeks is almost perfectly absent,

evidence of her brother's distinctive presence, his essence—evidence that this was his office, his life, and his alone. Her parents have already been through, of course, and received permission to cart off a few things. They flew home ahead of her this morning, toting an extra suitcase full of stuff. That, plus their son's remains, or what remains of them—a little pot of teeth and ashes, less the spoonfuls ladled out to various friends and lovers.

"I feel so *strange* around these people," her mother had murmured to Jan, nursing a sherry at the boisterous wake. Trying to be open and honest, just as Jan has always begged her to do.

"I didn't know you were uncomfortable around *doctors*, Mom," Jan had replied, willfully misinterpreting, despising herself for the snarkiness.

There's just one thing, a leather jacket hanging on the back of the office door. Black with hardware highlights—classic Lance. But why is it here? Why didn't Lance take it with him that last night? And what if he had? Or what if he'd returned for it, ridden the elevator back up here instead of wandering coatless out into that autumn evening? Would this have been enough to knock the cosmos off kilter, nudge it onto an alternate course, a future in which the bullet would have passed right through him without puncturing his lung?

Jan takes the jacket from its hook, slips into it. Once again she's startled by how big her little brother grew to be—stretching out her arms, scarecrow straight, she can barely wriggle her fingers free of the sleeves. She hugs herself, presses her face into the jacket's lining. She inhales her brother's scent, sweat, leather, some musky new cologne. Hungry for him now she digs into his pockets. Matches. Coins. Two opera tickets—*Dido and Aeneas*—for tonight.

Jan shudders. She shrugs out of the jacket, returns it to its hook. "*More I would*," she sings softly to herself, "*but death invades me*." She steps over to the window, peers out at the garbage-strewn alley, the gap-toothed skyline that's just swallowed the sun. *Dido*—when did Lance's taste get so refined? Why didn't he let her know about it, why didn't he share these things? Why did he ever leave his family in the first place, to come out here alone?

There's a gentle knock at the door. Jan turns. Detective Hayashi, the young man in charge of the investigation, edges into the office. He's been out there rummaging through files since before she arrived, hunting for clues, presumably, cryptic appointments, cases gone bad.

"Ms. Parks—"

"Jan," says Jan.

"Jan," says Detective Hayashi. "I'm finished here for now, I need to lock up. Would you like a little more time, or . . . ?"

"No. I'm ready."

"Do you mind, then . . . could I ask you a couple of questions?"

"Of course."

"I know this is difficult," says the detective, "especially since you and your brother have lived at such a distance from one another for so long."

Jan says, "Five years." She gives a little hiccup, a little huff of grief, as close as she's yet come to crying. Detective Hayashi reaches out, touches her shoulder. It's a practiced gesture, almost ceremonial—he might be knighting her, or absolving her of her sins.

"But you obviously knew him really well," he says. "Can you think of any enemies Lance may have had?"

Time for Jan to laugh now—her harshest, most high-pitched laugh, the one she hates. "I'm sorry," she says, as soon as she's able to rein herself in. "You're serious."

Detective Hayashi grins, and then instantly corrects himself with a frown—mask of comedy, mask of tragedy. There's something rather dramatically odd about him anyway, the little round head atop the gangly body. A hybrid, surely, a mutt. Lance always fell for mutts.

"Okay," she says. She starts ticking items off on her fingers. "Well, he did abortions of course, so any number of pro-lifers wanted him dead. And he assisted at a whole bunch of suicides.

And he was an environmentalist, a serious one. I don't mean he rode his bike to work every once in a while, I mean he was out there chaining himself to things all the time, sabotaging things. He was gay. He was promiscuous—he never figured out that condoms didn't make that safe. Says Miss Abstemious here." She shrugs. "But you know all this. Is there anything else?"

"No," says Detective Hayashi. "I mean, well, yes. But nothing official. Are you . . . do you by any chance like opera?"

He lifts the jacket from the back of the door, slings it over his shoulder. The way Lance would have done it, she thinks—that same delicate abandon. She's ready to cry now—this could get messy—but there isn't time. He's opening the door, waiting for her to step through.

sTump

I'm downtown with Patty, my seven-year-old, when she springs the question. The question I've dreaded for so long now, or one of them, anyway. Sara's with Jason, the baby. Sara has breasts so she gets to stay home and experience a frigging miracle while I shop.

We've shrugged and scowled our way through six stores so far, Patty and I, in search of the perfect pair of sneakers. Patty has flat feet—got them from her mom, along with the chutzpah and the high-voltage hair—so these sneakers have to be substantial in the arch. They also have to creep in somewhere under seventy-five bucks, with tax—this from yours truly, the gruff, near-impotent voice of reason in our household. Patty's main stipulation is that they be pale blue. We've located a royal blue pair, so far, a navy blue pair, and a bizarre neon blue pair. Nothing doing. Patty'll go barefoot before she'll settle for anything other than pale blue.

Finally, in the window of Kids R Worth It—why do I feel like bludgeoning somebody all of a sudden?—we spot a minuscule pair of pale blue runners. We rush in, only to be ruined by the news that this style is available solely in tiny sizes.

"Maybe pale blue is more of a baby thing," I muse. "Big kids like you seem to be into stronger colours."

Patty doesn't deign even to acknowledge this lame effort.

Back out on the street I'm starting to fade. I'd kill for a coffee and a croissant. Patty, meanwhile, is just hitting her stride. She looks fresh, optimistic—Edmund Hillary on day one out of base camp.

"Quarter for a cup of coffee, chief?"

He's got a ball cap upturned in one hand, weighted down with a couple of dimes, a couple of nickels. His other hand is missing—missing all the way up to the shoulder, as a matter of fact. It's a chilly day—Patty's submitted to scarf and toque—but his stump is exposed. It looks like a giant knuckle, chapped, inflamed. He waves it at us, as though to embellish some story, emphasize some elusive point we've failed to fathom. "Sound of one hand," I'd murmur to Sara if she were with us, and she'd flash me her sad smile. But she isn't.

We've barely left the guy behind when Patty springs her question. Actually, what she does is she goes quiet—the question's there in the way she doesn't ask it. Or questions, maybe I should say. *Why did he call you "chief"? What happened to his arm? Why couldn't they put it back on? Why did you say you were sorry? Didn't you used to have a pair of blue pants like that? What would happen if my arm came off? Can you die from having your arm come off? What happens when you die? How does he tie up his shoes? Why doesn't he get those Velcro ones? How much money do you think he makes? How much money is a lot of money? What does he do when it rains? Can I have my allowance? Doesn't his little arm thingy get cold? Why doesn't he put a mitten on it? Or a hat? Do arms ever grow back? Do you think he's a father? Why doesn't he play a drum or something, like the kids do? Do you think nose rings are gross? Do you think he used to play the guitar? Or the banjo? Or the ukulele? Which is bigger, a banjo or a ukulele?*

"A banjo," I say.

"What?" says Patty.

I steer her into the next department store, another long shot. There they are, a pair of pale blue sneakers featured prominently in a display case by the door. They glow, these sneakers, they pulsate like an empty summer sky. They feature Hydro-Shocks and a patented Tectonic Arch. They look just about Patty's size, maybe a little room to grow. They're marked down twenty percent. They're a miracle, a message from God, as perfect and perfectly devoid of meaning as every other.

"There," I say, once they're bought and bagged. "Now home."

"What did I do?" says Patty.

feeleRs

"An entomologist, did you say?" says Harlan, incredulous. He's been here at the Bougainvillea Resort and Spa about an hour and already something wild is happening to him. "From the Greek *entomon*, insect? From the neuter of *entomos*, cut up, from *temnein*, to cut?"

"Um, I guess so," says the woman standing next to him—head cocked, arms akimbo—before the rack of brochures. "Bugs."

"Because you see I'm an etymologist," says Harlan. "Entomologist, etymologist, don't you think that's kind of uncanny?"

"Etymologist?" says the woman. "Like, words?"

"Right," says Harlan. "From the Greek *etymon*, from *etymos*, true, and of course *logion*, diminutive of *logos*"—no way to stop himself when he's wound this tight—"a saying, especially a saying of Christ's. Can I buy you a drink?"

"Sure," says the woman. "My name's Miriam."

"Harlan," says Harlan.

They place their orders—gin and tonic for Harlan, virgin Caesar for Miriam ("Ha!" from Harlan)—and wander out onto a little patio overlooking one of the pools. It's dusk, but birds still sing—mockingbirds, presumably, as promised by the resort's literature. Poring over the pamphlet at home a few weeks ago, Harlan strove to imagine the mockingbird's evening cry. He failed. Failure comes easily to Harlan. Most recently he failed at marriage. This trip, an impulsive purchase which will max out all three of his credit cards, was inspired by the arrival of his divorce papers.

Harlan and Miriam take seats at a little table by a potted palm with a view of the setting sun—a hot-pink smear over the tennis courts—cross their legs and start chatting. During their conversation they discover all sorts of things about one another. They discover that they're both from Toronto, that they've both just arrived at the Bougainvillea Resort and Spa, that they were both on the same flight, Harlan in seat 7E (seven, coincidentally, being the most blessed of all numbers according to the faith of her fathers, to say nothing of her mothers), Miriam in seat 34D (Harlan's eyebrows going up here—the figure's just about right, judging by the trippy distortion of the stripes on her blouse). They discover that Harlan had the chicken, Miriam the pasta. They discover that neither of them ever goes on a vacation like this, or has a spouse, or a child.

Inevitably, though, the things they discover about one another are way outnumbered by the things they don't discover about one another. For example, Miriam doesn't discover that as a boy Harlan indulged in a dark practice for which he later coined the term *entomosadism*—yanking not the limbs but the antennae, the fine feelers, from various creepy-crawlies. Nor does she discover that Harlan is here recovering from his botched marriage, a knowledge which, a couple of months down the road, will fill her with remorse. Harlan, for his part, doesn't discover that as a girl Miriam consistently misheard the Torah passage, "I will make him an help meet for him," (God taking pity on his lonesome man of clay), as "I will make him an elk meat form." Worse, perhaps, he doesn't discover that Miriam is here recovering (still) from the loss of her child, a baby girl known as Toots who died at the age of three hours, before she could get herself a proper name—all of this nine years ago now, when Miriam was twenty-five years old. A couple of months down the road this knowledge will inspire in him a sense of awe for the human heart—Miriam's, for example, and his own—the depth to which it can be damaged, the weird miracle of its healing.

For the next ten days, though, the two will flourish in a state of blissful ignorance of these and umpteen other details. They'll come to adore one another's little quirks, the affected way Harlan has of twirling his walking stick—a brass-and-mahogany heirloom from somebody else's family he scooped at a swap meet years ago, and has never since gone without—or the way Miriam bares her teeth like a baboon on the cusp of each orgasm.

"Love," Harlan will sigh, "from the Old English *lufu*, akin to the Latin *lubere*, to please."

A couple of months from now, when Miriam dumps Harlan, she'll do it with a gift, a plastic terrarium which will appear, at first, to be bereft of life. Taped to the glass will be this note:

> *Harlan, my dear, this is a carausius morosus, a "walking stick"—thought you'd enjoy the word play. I've named her Toots, after the little girl I lost many years ago. I'm sorry I could never bring myself to tell you. She likes brambles, please, fresh every day. She'll have babies, even though she has no mate. Do you know the word parthenogenesis? Of course you do. I'm afraid that pill I popped every morning wasn't THE pill, as I let you assume, it was just something for my allergies. Again, I'm sorry. I wanted your height, and your intellect—a flair for the humanities to balance out my science. And anyway I*

liked you, I really did. I swear to God I won't come after you for child support. Please just forgive me, if you can, and then forget us. Love, Babs

Eventually Harlan will spot her, a greenish bug about the length of his pinky, a stick with six stick-legs and two antennae. "Hello, Toots," he'll say. "Parthenogenesis," he'll say, "from the Greek *parthenos*, virgin, and Latin *genesis*. Virgin birth, baby." Harlan will wonder whether he's ever had anything irreplaceable, whether he's lost it. Brambles? he'll wonder. Where the hell am I going to find brambles in this town?

female drunKen immortal fist

I was spoiled I suppose, Pauline, my first, having been a princess. But Ben's a handful by anybody's standard. Colic, they call it, in other words they haven't the faintest why your child bawls like a branded calf, why he won't stop. If he isn't hot and he isn't cold and he isn't wet and he isn't hungry and he isn't tired then there has to be something else bugging him, something from before, something he brought with him when he came. You'd better go back and find out what, or he'll never be anything to you but a question mark.

Pauline, as I say, had been royalty, and in Arabia, where they treat their royalty right. Mrs. Grainger did the reading that time too. She kept oohing and aahing at all Pauline's fine things, the endless palace she moved through—"heaven, if heaven were a maze," as Mrs. Grainger put it. It made me wonder what Pauline must have done last time around to drop down so far in the world, to wind up with a single mom destined to be a single mom a second time. Then again, it can't have been so bad. She's never been hard up for love, or for anything much else either. Maybe she was a touch testy with one of her slaves one day. Maybe she played around on her prince.

Ben had just turned two months when I took him to see Mrs. Grainger, in her little apartment there above the karate studio. It's a wonder she can hear herself think, let alone tune in to past lives, what with all that racket from down below. The thumping and the crying out—like twenty men gutshot all at once, over and over again. *Heeaaiihhhh!* It was the cheap rent that drew her to the place but it's the name in the window that keeps her there. Stenciled in red beneath the Oriental hashmarks, *Siang Chung Li Chien.* Female Drunken Immortal Fist is what it means, according to Mrs. Grainger, and she should know, she speaks pretty much every tongue. To her it's not just a sign but a *sign.* "That's what it's like," she told me the time I took Ben, "when I'm in that other place. It's like I'm being crushed by an immortal fist, a drunken immortal fist, a female drunken immortal fist. Soft, but so powerful." She held up her own fleshy paw, slowly scrunching her napkin—she serves tea and Oreos when you first arrive. "I feel wrung out for days," she said. "Which is why I'm upping it to seventy-five dollars."

You couldn't hear them carrying on down below that day anyway, what with Ben howling at the top of his lungs. If he had words, what would he say? Would he be able to tell us his story? Not likely. Here's my theory, my theory is that you lose your last life as soon as you have a way of capturing it. Actually it's Mrs. Grainger's theory, but I agree. It's like a dream slipping away just as you reach for it.

I could tell from Mrs. Grainger's expression it was bad news. With Pauline she'd had on this fierce, euphoric face, like a baby the first time it latches on. With Ben it was like she was sucking cold water from a bottle, when she'd been expecting warm milk. Angry, afraid. She was holding Ben's hand—she always does that, for contact—and I was terrified she'd immortal fist him she got so worked up.

"A great ship," she moaned, tilting her fuzzy head back and swiveling it—a toddler scanning a crowd for its mom. But eyes closed. "A great ship in shallow water, scraped, scrapped . . . Hungry, so hungry . . . Hot sand, hot steel . . . A flame, a torch . . ." This went on for quite a while. Brief images, just like with Pauline. You only get glimpses in that other place—I picture a dance lit by a strobe light.

Mrs. Grainger was pretty discombobulated by the time she'd done with the vision. She hustled us off in a big hurry, giving Ben a rough hug on his way out the door. Next day I gave the bits of information to Lois Rees, my best friend at the hospital where we both clean. It was Lois who first brought me to see Mrs. Grainger. Lois was a multiple rapist last time around, which pretty much explains her relationship issues. For a long time she tried to get me to go, but I never wanted to know about myself. Maybe I was a man too, in my last life, a philanderer dumping moms and tots all over the blessed place. Maybe that's why this has happened to me, but what am I supposed to do about it now? No, it wasn't until the kids that I got curious.

As I say, I gave Lois the information about Ben and she plugged it into the Internet. No children—she spends half her life on that machine. She put in "ship" and "scrap" and "torch" and came up with something called "ship breaking." It's done in India, apparently, in a particular place where the tide's just right. The whole world sends its old wrecks there to be beached and busted up by hand. Thousands of men work there and live in little hovels, and they die on the job—crushed or burnt or poisoned by the disgusting fumes—or they die at home, of TB, leprosy, some disease we cured eons ago. Which one took Ben, I wonder?

Or Balik, I suppose he was. Bharati.

Lois printed out a picture for me that I carry around now in my purse, to help me remember. There's a long line of skinny brown men in loincloths shouldering a heavy rope—they look like hydro poles supporting a power line, or slaves all shackled at the neck. The line dwindles into the distance, where the rope must be hooked up to some piece of steel or machinery. The sand around the men smoulders, with burning oil I suppose—if you found this picture in the back of your Bible it would say under it, "Hell." Further off you see ships squatting in the shallow water, grey corpses with great slabs missing, as though they've been picked over by giant gulls.

It's a relief in a way, to know for sure what's tormenting him. The first thing I did was I stripped off the wallpaper in his bedroom, blue battleships if you can believe it, with grey gulls on a white background. And I switched to sponge baths, to give him a break from the water for a while. I'm more patient with him now, too, when he fusses at the breast, or when he wakes up frantic in the night. I think he's already a little better. We're finally getting some sleep.

To cover all the bases I've also cut dairy out of my diet, and anything else that might disagree with Ben—onions, cabbage, cauliflower. And I've got him on special drops, a concoction made for colic, with wild yam and chamomile and goodness knows what else. At night I run the vacuum cleaner in his room. It seems to soothe him—reminds him he's here, I suppose, that he's escaped from that awful place. It's more than I can stand, to imagine him there. Or to imagine what he must have done to deserve it.

avaLanche

T

Fuck. Why can I never remember this? Is it Anger and then Guilt, or Guilt and then Anger? Dr. De Witt would have straightened this out for me, or no, he'd have twisted it into a question. "Why do you think it's so important for you to experience these affects in a particular order? Hmm?" An order *he himself had imposed on me.* This was one of his favourite tricks, he'd let me know what was normal and then he'd make me feel like a freak for being so hung up about it. Should have throttled the son of a bitch while I had the chance.

I guess you'd have to say I'm in Anger just at the moment. For one thing, what kind of vicious, fucked-up world would make a person go through five stages of grief? Three stages aren't enough, somehow? Four? No, let's make the sorry bastards go through *five* stages of grief every time they're bereft of something. Limb, lover, doesn't matter what they've lost, they do all five stages. And let's make the whole thing so bloody convoluted they never know for sure which of the five stages they're at.

Take me. I'm angry right now, incredibly angry—but couldn't this anger be a ruse? A feint? Couldn't this anger just be a fancy way of refusing to look at the truth? Truth's never been my strong suit, as Evangeline was forever pointing out. But that would mean I haven't made it to Anger at all, that I'm gridlocked back at square one, Denial. Anyway, I'm angrier with myself than with anyone else, my anger's all turned inward—and isn't anger turned inward just Guilt, the stage before Anger? Or the stage after Anger . . .

Fuck.

Speaking of anger, I'm deeply pissed off with myself for not seeing Dr. De Witt more often while he was around. I was trying to wean myself, or at least I was trying to give myself the impression that I was trying to wean myself. Actually *terminating the therapy*, as Dr. De Witt would occasionally put it—a hollow threat meant to keep me off balance, shades of Evangeline—was the furthest thing from my mind. And now suddenly, he's gone. Suddenly and absolutely. I can't believe it.

Denial.

Or yeah, Guilt. Sure, I'm feeling more than a little guilty about my treatment of Dr. De Witt. Would it have killed me to interrupt my neurotic rant now and then to check on him? "So Dr. De Witt, how's the little woman? How are you sleeping these nights, hounded by a pack of emotional midgets like me?" If one, just *one* of us had taken a little interest in Dr. De Witt he mightn't have needed a skiing vacation. If he hadn't needed a skiing vacation he wouldn't have been buried by that avalanche, and if he hadn't been buried by that avalanche I'd still have somebody to torture with all my troubles.

I've been to the bookstore, by the way, Nevil's New And Used, just around the corner from Dr. De Witt's office. I thumbed through each and every volume on the grief shelf. Nevil's wife kept throwing me dirty looks—thought she could guilt me into whipping out my wallet. If she'd had any idea how many sessions I've put in on my guilt issues she'd have saved herself the trouble. People have written profusely, copiously, as it turns out, on coping with the loss of a parent. A grandparent? No problem. A sibling? A child? A fetus? A pet? A friend? A lover? A spouse? A complete stranger? Got it covered. But a shrink? Nothing. It's shrinks that write this stuff, they have no idea what happens to us when they kick. There are reams of words of wisdom on dealing with death by AIDS, by cancer, by heart attack, by embolism and aneurysm, by car crash, by murder, by suicide (how is it that any of us are actually *alive?*). But death by avalanche? Complete silence. Needless to say I slotted all the books back onto the shelf in the wrong order. I'm in Anger, right? Just before Guilt, or just after—I was so pissed off I forgot to look.

I could just grab myself another psychiatrist, I know that. But remember, it's backfired once already. The whole point of going to Dr. De Witt was to get over my tendency to become dependent. I was stuck in Guilt (or it might have been Anger) about losing Evangeline. "I swear to Christ I'll never get hurt again," I told Dr. De Witt at our first session. He smiled, checked his appointment book. He asked me, "It's been *how* long since you last slept?" So began our *grief work*, as he called it. Ten months later I could feel myself just beginning to make progress when Evangeline rang up for her Emmylou Harris albums.

I don't have to crawl.
I can just walk away.
I don't have to crawl.
I don't have to crawl.

There's simply no limit to what a person can lose.

The goal, I think, is to sink as rapidly as possible into Depression. That way you have some slight hope of creeping your way into Acceptance before the axe falls again. Sinking into a depression has never been a big problem for me in the past, but this time I have to make it through Denial, Anger, and Guilt—or Denial, Guilt, and Anger, whatever—in order to earn myself the privilege. The whole thing infuriates me so much I don't see how I'll ever get as far as Depression. It's depressing.

I called Evangeline last night. I said, "Sing me that other song, same album. How does it go?"

"Oh, 'How High the Moon,'" she said. "You know me and lyrics. But . . ." And she la-la-la-ed it for me, long and loud.

"Thanks," I said. "That was beautiful." Though to tell the truth she's practically tone-deaf. "Is it a question, do you think? 'How high the moon,' is it a question?"

"No," she said. "I don't think so."

sHroud

T

Jackie says, "What do you see?" She holds up a set of pajama bottoms, deep burgundy, and waves them at him bullfighter style.

Bill paws the floor with his one sock-foot, the other foot already stuffed into a black rubber boot. "Neil's PJs?" he says. "And by the way, where is the little goofball? He was supposed to give me this whole Sunday afternoon. What's the point of having a son if you still end up—"

"No, *look*." Jackie uncreases the fabric to reveal a large white flaky stain.

So. The boy has turned, presto chango, into a man. Bill recalls—briefly revisits—the night he himself first awoke in the midst of that sloppy paroxysm, on the top bunk of the basement room he shared with his kid brother. In his dream Ms. Laliberté, her turquoise sweater a wavy lake he longed to fall into, fell instead onto him, overturning his school desk, wriggling against his lap. "*Guillaume,*" she murmured into the giddy cup of his ear, "*s'il vous plaît, Guillaume. Répétes avec . . . moi.*" The first little death. And lying there afterwards, soggy, scared—and reassured, for once, by the faint sleepy snuffling from down below.

"Um, Bill?" says Jackie. "Hello?" The washing machine behind her, its lid propped open, grumbles in that I'm-going-to-*cost*-you tone of voice it's recently adopted.

"Yeah, I'm here," says Bill.

"So, do you see it?" She hoists the bottoms up a little higher. It occurs to Bill that his wife has Ms. Laliberté's mouth—wide and lippy, with the hint of an overbite.

"Sure," he says, "of course I see it. I guess he'll be wanting extra allowance now, for condoms." Bill jams his other foot into its boot, experiencing a pleasant little buzz of fatherly pride.

Jackie shakes her head, incredulous. "When was the last time you did laundry, Bill? Never mind. I'm saying look at the shape. What is it? *Who* is it?"

Bill blinks. "You mean, Neil's already . . . ?"

Jackie brandishes the pajamas at him again.

Obediently, Bill scrunches up his eyes—just about due for readers—and strives to decipher the stain. Actually, it's pretty obvious. The hippie hair hanging down in those two limp hanks, the way it does in all the pictures, and on the famous shroud. The long, mournful, messianic face, squared off by the beard. The deep-set eyes under their dark arches. It's Jesus Christ Almighty.

"Amazing, eh?" says Jackie. "You can even see the wrinkles, like when he was a pup, when you and Neil picked him out." And she turns, tosses the bottoms into the sloshing machine.

"Incredible," says Bill, and opens the back door.

He finds the rake where Neil discarded it earlier in the afternoon, rotten kid, beside a molehill of moulding leaves in the centre of the back yard. There's a mist in the air, not quite rain. Boris is busy with a scent trail over by the compost bin—rat, raccoon.

"Boris!" Bill shouts at the top of his lungs. The old hound raises his head, looks off uncertainly in the wrong direction.

"Boris! Over here, boy!"

This time Boris locates the source of the faint sound, comes loping. Bill squats and takes the grizzled head in his hands. The shoulder-length ears, the long square muzzle, the dark alleys of the eyes just beginning to frost over, to disappear behind the finest of veils. Uncanny.

Bill lifts one silky ear. He calls into it, "Let's go in, boy. Let's surprise her."

dear Ann

I got married last year to a wonderful man. I'll call him "Pete," even though his name is Brian. I was on a temp assignment with his pharmaceutical firm when we fell in love. He proposed and I accepted, positive we could get past the one big barrier to our happiness. I'm talking about our difference of faith. You see, I'm a Kabbalist, Pete's an Alchemist. That shouldn't matter though, should it, Ann? Nothing should matter except our love for one another, right?

But he smells. Not Pete, Pete doesn't smell, but his experiments, his "sublimations," as he says. Pete has his lab in the basement of our bungalow (right where our family room ought to be, by the way), so vapours come wafting up through the vents—I live in a cloud of air freshener shot through with sulfur. I worship in the living room right above him, and it's no joke, meditating on the *Zohar*, say, *The Book of Splendour*, or reciting the divine names while you're gasping for breath.

Maybe I'm being unfair. After all, if Pete's experiments ever work out, if he does manage to turn our garbage into gold, we'll be rich. Hey, I'd love an SUV as much as the next person. But Ann, is that all there is to life?

Plus, there are the pictures. I thought it was up to the wife to decorate the house, Ann. My mother decorated hers. But Pete has his dreadful iconography up everywhere. For above the mantel I had in mind this lovely piece of my Grandma's needlework, of the Ten *Sefirot*—the emanations from the *Ein Sof*, of course, God in His radical transcendence (I'm sure you know all this stuff, Ann, but some of your readers may not). Now Pete has this gigantic engraving up there, of a naked body—I can't say "man" or "woman" because this body has both sets of privates—with a huge pregnant belly and two "heads," a sun and a moon. You'd think one transformation symbol would be as good as the next, wouldn't you? But I'm sorry, I miss the *Sefirot*.

Then there's the bedroom. Over our Posturepedic he's got a whole series of pictures with titles like, *King and Queen fall in love on the backs of two lions, emblems of their sulfurous and incestuous passion*, and, *King and Queen engage in birdlike intercourse, pecking each other to death while fusing into one.* I'm no prude, Ann, but seriously.

Mom's worried sick, of course. She's just a sweet old-fashioned Kabbalist, is all she is. She doesn't need this. She was here the other day and wouldn't you know it, Pete started in about us all being reborn, about how we'll have to die to ourselves, return to the original chaos of the *prima materia.* He just kept on about the *prima materia*, whatever that is. Mom smiled and sipped her tea, but I know she was terrified.

Ann, I'm trying to be a good wife, to pursue *tikkun*, the healing, the holiness that will bring us the Messiah. Honestly, though, I'm at my wits' end. What am I to do?

Yours,

Puzzled on the Material Plane

Dear *Puzzled*,

Have you tried an air purifier? Some brands are very good. If you put one in each room, you'll be surprised how much it will help with the vapours from your husband's hobby.

By the way, when you're having company over, mix up a little butter and cinnamon in a pan and pop it into a low oven. Your house will be filled with harmony.

darK beast

“Hey, I have a confession to make too,” says Danny. “How about that!” He’s backed way down to the other end of the couch, well clear of Ruth’s reach. He’s cried already—a relatively brief spritz he was able to mop up swiftly with one sleeve of his sweatshirt—and he’s desperate not to cry again.

Not crying is more of a challenge for Danny than it is for most men of his age. Danny cries when your average thirty-six-year-old man would get away with clearing his throat, or feigning a little hay fever. Danny cries when the father on the credit card commercial flies home from a business trip for his son’s first hockey game, not because Danny’s own father did or didn’t do this kind of thing (like most fathers, Danny’s sometimes did and sometimes didn’t do this kind of thing), and not because Danny wishes he had a son of his own to foul up his busy schedule (although this desire does in fact tweak him more and more often these days), but because Danny suffers from a condition known as epiphora, or excessive tearing, his lachrymal glands overactive, his lachrymal canaliculi—the little canals meant to siphon away his tears—undersized. His chances of extracting himself from this situation without a total meltdown are slim to none. Still, gotta try.

"I should have told you this ages ago," he continues. "I should have told you this that first night, that very first night we met. God, is it six years ago now?"

"Seven," says Ruth. "But Danny, I think we should be—"

"Remember, at Hung and Kit's place?" says Danny. "We were all drinking martinis, the whole crowd of us." As he speaks he joggles his head ever so slightly to the rhythm of the song on the stereo, the sort of sad, twangy thing Ruth's suddenly so partial to these days. Another sign, he supposes, another missed signal. "Somebody had brought over this huge bottle of vermouth, and the right glasses and everything, with the long stems. Olives."

"Liz," says Ruth. "Liz brought all the stuff, I know because I came with her. But Danny—"

"So we were all drinking martinis," says Danny, "all of us except Kit. Kit said she never drank martinis, remember? She told us martinis were a bit of a *bête noire* for her." The streetlight just outside their apartment window—the CM as they've come to call it, the Ceaseless Moon—suddenly clicks on, conjuring dark doubles of them on the hardwood floor. Ruth stretches out a hand. Danny withdraws even further, barnacling himself to the arm of the couch. "Everybody laughed," he says, "we were halfway drunk already and for some reason it was incredibly funny, and then people started slipping *bête noire* into all their sentences. *Bête noire* this and *bête noire* that. And after about ten minutes—"

"It wasn't ten minutes, Danny. For goodness' sake, it was maybe five."

"Okay, five minutes," says Danny. "After five minutes you

suddenly piped up and said, 'What's a *bête noire?*' That whole time you didn't even know what a *bête noire* was, and then all of a sudden you came out with it, 'What's a *bête noire?*' I already liked you—which was Kit's little plan, of course—but at that moment, my God."

"Danny, I want to tell you how it happened," says Ruth. "I want you to understand that I never—"

"You were suddenly so vulnerable," says Danny. "That's what got me, that you were willing to make yourself so vulnerable. And I let you."

"Sweetheart—"

"Because here's the thing," says Danny. "Here's the part I've never told you before, never once in all the times I've kidded you about this. Here's the thing. I didn't know what a *bête noire* was either." Danny makes a fist of his right hand, punches himself in the thigh. Hard. "It wasn't just you, you see? I didn't know what a *bête noire* was either. I could never get those little foreign phrases straight. Was it a final stroke? No, that's a *coup de grâce.* Was it something that doesn't follow? No, that's a *non sequitur*, and anyway what does a martini follow from, or not follow from?"

"Danny—"

"*Mise en scène?*" says Danny. "*Dolce vita?* I wanted so much to impress you. I lied right off the bat, that's the very first thing I ever did with you, was I lied. I lied by letting you think you were the only one who was in the dark. 'Dark beast,' that's what it means, *bête noire*. It's the thing you really hate because of how much it can hurt you."

At some point he must have started crying again because he's tasting salt, and Ruth is advancing on him down the couch. "Danny, I swear to God—"

"Was this the first time?" says Danny. "Because you know it's weird, I'm having this *déjà vu*." He unfolds one leg, lashes out with it, flipping the oak coffee table onto its back. Books and magazines go skidding across the floor. "Yeah, I'm pretty sure I've done that before," he says, still gushing tears. "Did you plan it or was it *ad hoc*? Did you do it indoors or *al fresco*? You see, Ruth, I know them all, now. Now I know them all."

cOnversion

T

It was my first time up in the air since 9/11, since the day my wife and I dashed home from work—leaving Gillian where she was at Toddler Town—to be together as those two planes plowed into those two towers again and again and again. I was seated early in one of the back rows so I played the game of guessing which of the passengers shuffling down the aisle towards me would turn out to be my neighbour. Bracing myself, I picked the giant jolly guy in the leather vest, the lanky Jesus look-alike with the wheeze and the laptop, the blue-rinsed lady who squinted and scowled at her boarding pass as though it were rife with grammatical errors, or obscenities. But it was a petite, pasty young woman—twenty-fivish, say, a little more than half my age—who eventually excused herself and pressed past me to the window seat. Dark, spiky hair, a little jewel nestled in the cleft of one pale nostril. Scruffy, but confidently middle-class in the way she carried herself.

"Hi," I said.

"Hi," she said. A girlish smile, unguarded. It gave me that little rush again, that bittersweet infusion of relief and regret I get every time I'm reminded of how absolutely asexual I've become to these young women. This, even as I took note of the swath of soft skin on the inside of her arm just above the enchanting hinge of her elbow.

"Hi," I said again.

This was the extent of our conversation for the first fifteen minutes or so, maybe half an hour, until we'd leveled off at thirty-five thousand feet, Montreal dwindling in the darkness behind us, New York City an hour or so ahead. I was sipping from one of those little plastic wine glasses, worrying about my white shirt, wondering what the devil had possessed me to order red. I craned my neck a couple of times, trying to get a bead on our sole Arabic passenger—a woman, thank the lord, and too frumpy to look like much of a fanatic. I didn't want anybody freaking out, slowing things down at the other end with any security shenanigans. Periodically I flipped a page of Pascal's *Pensées*. Most of my attention was reserved, though, for my neighbour's glossy fashion magazine. I'd get a waft every now and then of some come-hither scent as she passed a perfume ad, the odd sidewise glimpse of ribbed cleavage on yet another scrawny model.

If I was fascinated by my little friend's magazine, I wondered, was it possible she was the tiniest bit intrigued by my book? Impressed, even? A hefty thing, after all, and bilingual to boot, with rich creamy pages and a puckish portrait of the great man on its cover. It had belonged to my father, a far more reflective and devout individual than I'd ever pretended to be. Until that evening. I made sure to angle the book so my friend could appreciate the profundity of its font. I scowled and nodded, as though being won over by some particularly dazzling stream of ratiocination. There was no way for her to know I couldn't decode much of the French—as I'm sure she could have done, a classy kid like that from our schizoid patch of the planet—or that most of the English, too, was a perfect mystery to me. *Jesus will be in agony even to the end of the world. We must not sleep during that time.* Like many folks in the aftermath I'd felt the urge to ground myself, grab hold of faith, or allow myself to be grabbed by it. But this? *Too much and too little wine. Give him none, he cannot find the truth; give him too much, the same.* Too little, I judged, and took another sip.

Then, "What will you be doing in the Big Apple?" I said. What we're all longing for, as Pascal lamented, is diversion, distraction. "My name's Michael."

"Nina," said the girl. "Um, I'll be meditating."

"Meditating?" I was en route to my annual Insurers' convention, which promised to be extra harrowing this time around, what with the untallied billions being claimed in Manhattan. "That's a long way to go to meditate, isn't it? I mean, couldn't you have meditated at home?"

Again with the smile. "I'll be meditating with a whole bunch of other people," she said. "All of us are converging on Ground Zero. Consciousness is a field."

"Beg pardon?" Another sip.

"Consciousness is a field," she said. "Like magnetism? Or gravity? When you're upset or anxious or whatever it affects the whole field, the whole world. And the other way around. When you meditate, when you make yourself serene you, like, make the whole world serene. You make peace."

"Really," I said.

"Really." A child-like bob of the head. "They've done studies. When enough people—one percent I think it is—when enough people are meditating it starts to change everybody, even the people who aren't meditating. There's less crime, less illness, everything like that. And when a bunch of people meditate together it works even better."

"One percent?" I said.

"I'm pretty sure. So there'll be all these people from all

different races and religions, including Muslims, all meditating right there, right where it happened. Starting to, like, heal that."

"Eighty thousand," I said.

"I'm sorry?"

"Eighty thousand people," I said. "That's one percent. There are eight million people in New York City, give or take. One percent is eighty thousand. That's a lot of people meditating."

And I dumped the rest of my wine down the front of my shirt. The plane had bucked suddenly—a car speeding over a nasty bump—lifting us and then dropping out from under us. Gravity is a field.

"*Merde*," I snapped. Then, "Pardon my French."

There was a little ping. A woman's voice came on to advise us that we were experiencing turbulence, and to request that we observe the "fasten seatbelt" sign.

I looked down. The shirt was ruined, a great red continent swiftly forming on its ocean of white. And the girl, Nina, was clutching my hand.

"It's okay," I said reflexively. The power in those little fingers—it reminded me of the first time Gillian got hold of my thumb. "Really, it's okay. Statistically, you know, there are far fewer—"

Nina gave a little groan—mechanical, like a beam groaning under a weight it can scarcely support.

I said, "Right. You're right, let's talk about something else." The plane gave another jolt. Nina's eyes were closed—scrunched, really—so I took the opportunity to study her face. Pale, precise. A flapper's face, a face from a silent film. Indeed, as I looked on she began mutely moving her lips—some Sanskrit mantra, I assumed. "Do you know about Pascal?" I said. I rapped the cover of my book with the knuckles of my free hand. "A scientist, a mathematician, but also a very religious man." Another jolt. "Here's what he said, here's what Pascal said," I said. "Pascal said you're better off gambling that there is a God than that there isn't one. If you're wrong, so what? If there's no God, what does it matter? But if you're right, if there does turn out to be a God, then you've gained . . . everything."

I was seized, suddenly, with the need to persuade this girl, convert her—the need to seduce her into believing what no one could possibly believe. "Absolutely everything," I insisted. I prayed for the plane to buck again, to hit us even harder, and it did.

methoD

T

I took heart from the fact that Dali, too, was a virgin at twenty-four. It was at twenty-four that he met his muse, Gala Eluard, wife of surrealist poet Paul Eluard, and swiftly transformed her into the ex-wife of surrealist poet Paul Eluard. It didn't stop Dali wanking off, mind. Throughout his marriage he remained The Great Masturbator, as he dubbed himself in his autobiography and as he depicted himself in the superb painting of that name composed in the late nineteen twenties, the period during which he perfected his paranoiac-critical method. His what? His paranoiac-critical method. Oh.

At twenty-four, my own sexual accomplishments tallied up as follows: coitus—0, masturbation—4,015, by my best calculation, and counting. It seemed to me I showed great promise. My only niggler was that Max wasn't a poet. Could I consider Gabriella a proper muse if she was shacked up with a postman? And if not, what was the point of my stealing her away from him? But then I got it, man of *letters*. Ha. This was the paranoiac-critical method in action. Making connections, seeing signs where others saw nothing.

Like Gala, Gabriella managed to be boyish and womanish all at once. Like Gala, she was raven-haired, hot-tempered. Her gaze was mesmerizing, it could "pierce walls," as poor old Paul Eluard put it, referring to the love he'd soon lose. (Lesser men must sometimes suffer, so that fate may be fulfilled. Trust me.) "Dammit, Drew," Gabriella would snap, boring into me with those dark pile-driver eyes, "you forgot to clean up your dinner crap again."

"Sorry," is what I'd say, but here's what I'd be thinking: To *you* I dedicate my life's work.

Max and Gabriella were my landlords. Max was about ten years my senior, Gabriella five. I was renting their garage from them, a studio suite with a little bathroom but no kitchen—I did my cooking in the house. Each day I timed dinner so Gabriella was home from the campus, but Max had yet to stumble in from his *après*-route beer. Gabriella was completing a master's in social work. Empathy—a must-have in a muse.

Dali fell for Gala when he first glimpsed her from behind, her bare back bronzed against the shook cellophane of the sea, her soon-to-be-famous rump riding the air like a helium-filled balloon. I fell for Gabriella as she leaned over the breakfast table one morning—I'd come in to use the telephone—her flannel-enshrouded breasts swinging towards me with a mystifying weight.

Gabriella was saying, "You still call her Mommy?"

"My mother's just getting used to me not being around," I explained, still transfixed by those pendant parabolas. *Pendant Parabolas*—another title for my list of future works. Titles are a crucial aspect of any painter's craft. Consider Dali's *The Atavism of Dusk*, or *Atomic Leda*, or *Gala and the Angelus of Millet Preceding the Imminent Arrival of the Conic Anamorphoses*, or *Salvador Dali in the Act of Painting Gala in the Apotheosis of the Dollar, in Which Can*

Also Be Seen, on the Left, Marcel Duchamp Masked by Louis XIV Behind a Canopy in the Style of Vermeer, Which Is None Other Than the Invisible but Monumental Face of the Hermes of Praxiteles.

I couldn't rip my eyes away, so I closed them. "I'm trying to make her feel good," I said.

"Drew, don't you think maybe you should get out a little more?" said Gabriella. "I mean, what on earth do you *do* out there all the time?"

"My work's at a pivotal stage just now," I said, and I opened my eyes.

"Work?"

Five minutes later Gabriella, still in her nightie, was standing at the dead centre of my sanctum, cradling a mug of tea and staring around at the walls with a look of horrified wonder. "Are these really ... did you actually *paint* all these?" she said, and took a sip.

"Um, no," I said. "This is Dali. Salvador Dali? They're just posters."

"Oh. Right."

"I thought you were Spanish."

"My mother was Spanish. What's that one supposed to be?"

"That's the whole question, isn't it," I said. "It's called *The Metamorphosis of Narcissus.* Notice how the figure of Narcissus bent over the pool could also be a hand holding a cracked egg. And see, out of the crack comes a Narcissus flower. It's an amazing illustration of Dali's paranoiac-critical method."

"His what?"

"His paranoiac-critical method."

"Oh."

"Seeing different images in a single shape," I said. "He learned it from staring at water stains on a wall."

"Rorschach blot," said Gabriella.

"Exactly, that's exactly it. In an abstract shape you trace the outlines of your obsessions, in his case a horror of the body, the devouring woman. *Vagina dentatis.*"

"Uh-huh," said Gabriella. "What about that one?" She nodded in the direction of my easel bearing its blank canvas.

"'The only difference between me and a madman,' Dali once said," I said, "'is that I am not mad.'"

"Drew . . ." said Gabriella. "Drew, has it ever occurred to you that you could do anything at all with your life? That you're absolutely free?"

"No," I said, truthfully.

"Right now, you could do whatever you want."

"I want to paint you," I said. "All my life I've been preparing for this moment. Now I'm ready."

"Really?" said Gabriella. "Really, you want to paint *me?*" She didn't take a step, yet somehow she moved closer to me, reached out in my direction with her whole body, with her breath.

It may be stretching a point to call this a technique, a method. All I can tell you is that it worked for me.

near-death eXperience

"If she wakes up again—" says Jack, and smacks himself in the forehead. "Sorry, Boo, *when* she wakes up again."

"It's okay, Jack," says Boo. "I don't need you to pussyfoot."

"When she wakes up again," says Jack, "why don't you ask her? How many chances like this does a person get?"

"I'm not asking her," says Boo. "You can ask her yourself if you want to."

"But you're her daughter."

"Exactly," says Boo. "And anyway, it would be meaningless. What if she tells us there was a tunnel, a white light? What if she tells us Jesus was holding out his hand to her, that he, I don't know, poured her a glass of Bordeaux from the gash in his side? What would it prove?"

The woman in the hospital bed between them stirs, noisily smacking her lips. The left side of her face, Boo's side, contorts itself into a smirk or grimace—a baby with a bit of gas. The other half remains slack, devoid of expression. Eventually the whole face resumes its vapid repose. Boo's mother begins to snore, a juicy counterpoint to the soft chanting that issues from the portable tape deck on her bedside table.

Jack whispers, "She's been where we're all going, Boo. Aren't you the tiniest bit curious about what she's seen?"

"No. And anyway, I know what she's seen. She's seen what she's always seen when she closes her eyes. She's seen the inside of her head." Boo emits three shrill cries—it's as though she's been struck three times, swiftly and with great force, in the middle of her chest.

"Okay, Boo," says Jack. "Easy now."

An elderly gentleman in a green gown shuffles into the room shepherding an IV stand, a rictus of dismay disfiguring his deeply lined face. He peers at Jack and Boo, and then at Boo's mother. "You're in my bed," he croaks at her.

"Mr. Aziz," calls a nurse, catching up with him and gently turning him about. "Come on, Mr. Aziz, we've got a nice bed for you just down the hall." And to Jack and Boo, "Sorry about that."

Boo watches the pair effect a tentative tango out the door, then blows her nose. "Have you ever noticed," she says, and stops to blow it again. "Have you ever noticed that when a Christian gets ready to die he always meets Christ or Saint Peter or somebody? But when a Muslim gets ready to die he meets Mohammed, and when a Hindu gets ready to die he meets . . . I don't know, whoever the Hindus have? I mean, doesn't it strike you as a bit of a coincidence? Wouldn't you think that every once in a while—"

"Hon, let's keep it down just a bit, huh?"

"Fine," says Boo. "Fine, let's keep it down. Speaking of which, what is that you're playing?"

"It's a prayer," says Jack. "Cree, or maybe Chippewa, I forget. Anyway, it's supposed to be very healing, very soothing. I can't turn it down any lower."

"It's killing my head. Can we give it a rest?"

"Of course, hon." Jack reaches over to shut off the tape machine. "I just thought your mom—"

"You know, it's the weirdest thing," says Boo. "Mom's never learned a word of Cree, never learned a word of Chippewa. Can you believe that? And her a Scottish Presbyterian."

Abruptly Boo's mother pops up into a sitting position—a vampire at dusk fixing to emerge from its coffin. "Three seventy-five!" she exclaims in a gurgly, querulous voice, and slumps back again.

For a minute or so Jack and Boo simply stare at her, awaiting some further outbreak.

Jack finally whispers, "The price of a prom dress?"

"The heat of an oven," says Boo. "In about a minute she's going to get up and start fixing dinner. 'You two just relax,' she'll say. 'It's no bother.'"

Jack chuckles. "Boo, you've got to start letting this go."

"Do not."

Jack laughs again. "You know, I'll bet you two were lovers last time around. Yeah, only you were kept apart somehow, some sort of family squabble. Montagues and Capulets. Or you were chiefs of enemy tribes, hunting one another's heads. And it's just going to go on like this, Boo, lifetime after lifetime. Until you sort it out."

Boo closes her eyes, lowers her forehead to the bed's metal railing. This vision—an eternity of bickering with her mother—seems to be more than she can bear. "I don't *believe* any of this," she moans.

"I know you don't," says Jack. "But you've got to believe something, don't you? Say we had a kid, Boo. Just say we did. What would you tell him?"

"Him?" says Boo, raising her head.

"Or her."

"I'd tell her . . . I have no idea what I'd tell her," says Boo. "I'd tell her you can't believe anything, you can't count on anything.

I'd tell her the only thing you can count on is the absolute, the infinite. Anything less than that is a crock."

Jack says, "The absolute? The infinite?"

"I have no idea. Mom, I miss you, I do." Boo takes her mother's hand, kneads a knobby joint between her fingertips.

A nurse comes in, the same nurse responsible for the rescue of Mr. Aziz. "Sorry to interrupt," she says. And to Boo's mother, "Let's just check our blood pressure then, shall we?"

Boo says to her, "We did almost have a baby once, you know."

"Boo!" says Jack.

"Isn't that lovely," says the nurse, not really listening.

"Kim," says Boo. "Or Ryan."

"Excellent," says the nurse, unwrapping the gizmo from Boo's mother's arm. "You're doing so well."

iN translation

“Whatcha reading, sweetheart?” I say, meaning, *Come on, it’s late. How about closing that book, opening that nightie?*

“Just one of the essays in this feminist collection Barb gave me,” she says, meaning, *Get your own damn book. This is the first moment I’ve had to myself all day.*

“What’s it about, though, Marie-Claire?” I say, meaning, *After all these years, you know, the sound of your name still makes little purple blossoms start popping through my scalp.*

“Oh, nothing much,” she says, meaning, *If I wanted one of your rants on the decline of feminism, don’t you think I’d ask you for it? Now go to sleep.*

“Seriously, though,” I say. “Seriously, I want to know,” meaning, *I’ve been having that dream again, the last few nights. The one where that little bald Krishna keeps clapping my head between those two big cymbals? I’m afraid to sleep.*

"All right, all right," she says, "It's about, it's called, 'The Nipple As Signifier and Signified in French Canadian Art,' only in French of course," meaning, *It's way over your pretty little head, buster.*

"Interesting," I say, "so like, exploring the tension between nipple-as-source-of-pleasure and nipple-as-source-of-nourishment, woman as subject and as object?" meaning, *Well la-di-da.*

"Not exactly," she says, meaning, *How am I supposed to know what it's exploring, you won't let me read the bloody thing?*

"Aren't you feeling at all cuddly?" I say, meaning, *Don't let me forget my 9 o'clock with Bob Bennett, okay?*

"Yeah, maybe," she says, meaning, *Say* nipple *again.*

"Do you think the body is the ultimate source of all imagery?" I say, meaning, *Nipple.*

"*Peut-être*," she says, meaning, *I have my period.*

"Ah, who cares," I say, meaning, *Ah, who cares.*

aCrobat

“Bearded lady” would have been a bit of an exaggeration. She wasn’t much more bearded than he himself had been at seventeen, say, when his mother finally taught him to shave (his father having died in a plane crash at the time of his birth). It was fuzz, really, it was fluff. He took it for shadow when he first saw her from behind that day, bent low over her book at the Bright Side Café. The superb curvature of her cheekbone, the bronzed slope of her neck, the beaded string of her spine pressing through blue cotton. When she turned and fixed on him those big brown eyes—a child’s eyes, clear and quizzical, cradled in a fine woman’s face graced with manly tufts of hair—the gears of the universe slipped, the world came to a halt. She returned to her book. The gears re-engaged. The world started up again.

“Danielle Steel,” he said as he caught up to her outside the café. “I’m sorry, I couldn’t help noticing . . . Is she good?”

The woman slowed, shrugged. "It's just an escape. Romance."

"Love at first sight," he said, nodding. "Can I buy you a coffee? I mean, I know you just... My name's Anthony."

"Annie."

At first it was hard to concentrate, it was like talking to a man in the showers at the gym, fighting the urge to glance *down*. But they got on to her beard soon enough. Anthony had just explained how hard it was finding steady work as an architect. "And you?" he said. "What do you do for a living?"

"Phone sex," she said.

"Pardon me?"

"Phone sex. Guys call me up and have sex with me over the telephone." Her face suddenly went slack, dazed. "Oh, my God," she moaned. "I don't think I can ... it's too *big*."

He gave a great whoop of laughter. "Jesus, if they only... Oh."

"That's okay," she said. "I laugh about it too."

"I just meant—"

"Really, it's okay. That's maybe why I keep it, why I don't get it removed. It gives me something ... else."

"Sure," he said. "It makes you different. Everybody's got something special, something that makes them different. They should hang on to that thing."

She said, "So what about you? What's special?"

"Um, it's hard to talk about."

"Right," she said.

"I like to fly." It was all he could think of.

"Fly?" she said.

"In my dreams, I fly a lot."

"That's interesting," she said.

Later, in the front seat of her Toyota, they kissed. It was like nothing Anthony had ever experienced before, or rather it was like one thing he'd experienced before, it was like kissing the warm fuzzy head of an infant. That night they made love in Annie's bed. She was perfectly silent, but for one faint cry when he first entered her. In the morning there was a brownish smudge of blood on the pink sheet.

"I'm quitting today," she said. "I can't imagine doing that any more."

He stroked her cheek. "You're everything," he said. "You're everything I want. I want you." They made love again. He knew he'd never get enough.

He never did. A few months later he and Annie were living together when he began running into an old girlfriend down at the Bright Side, a freckled redhead with cheeks sleek as rayon. Things began to change. One night Anthony arrived home to find Annie clean-shaven, posing for him at the bedroom door in a bewilderingly complex set of lingerie.

"What's this?" he said.

"Come on, big boy," she said. "Take me *now*."

He did. In the morning she had a proper manly stubble.

"I'm the bearded lady," she said. "What are you?"

zeroes someone paiNted

"Josh, honey, how about you come down here and finish what you began!" This is what I'd be saying to him if I were a good mother, or rather this is what I'd be howling up the stairs at him—the music in his bedroom is already rocketing up the Richter scale. Our plates and cutlery and cups are neatly loaded into the dishwasher—pair-wise, like Noah's creatures—but the wok's still weltering in a sink full of greasy water. It isn't right.

I make it to the bottom of the stairs and draw breath before I stop to ask myself—as I'm constantly stopping to ask myself—who am I to be after him about this? Have I ever finished what I began? If I had, wouldn't I be a professor of biochemistry by now instead of a schoolbus driver? Wouldn't I be a size six instead of . . . well, instead of this size? Wouldn't I be the author of a science fiction trilogy set in a twenty-sixth-century post-apocalyptic world ruled over by orchids? Wouldn't my hands be registered as dangerous weapons? Wouldn't my mantel be crowded with photos of my Kenyan foster kid, my daybook a bedlam of appointments with volunteer boards? Wouldn't I have achieved a subtle, almost painfully profound understanding of Tolstoy and Proust by now, and be on to Faulkner and Woolf? Wouldn't I be plonking out stunningly original compositions (a tender Cecil Taylor) with a tight little trio on Friday and Saturday nights down at the Flatted Fifth? Wouldn't I have achieved *satori* and be taking on students in the spiritual discipline? Wouldn't I be married to the father of my son?

Not that Josh would hear me anyway, absorbed as he is in the impassioned rhymes of some pink-cheeked brat celebrating life in a black ghetto. I lean my forehead against the funny wooden ball we've got at the bottom of our banister, and I try to pick some words out of the grumbled incantation.

Something slash something something body in the ditch
With a something something something
And a something up that punk-ass nigga bitch . . .

"Not in this house, busta." This is what I'd say to him if I were a good mother. But by his age, of course, I was stupefying myself with the Stones, the Doors, Captain Beefheart, lord knows what else. I was dying for something so raunchy and outrageous it would make me feel real, make me believe there'd be life on the outside when I'd done my hard time in that appallingly safe little home. So I stay silent.

Suddenly the beat breaks off and Josh is clomping down the stairs at me—I'm gazing into the canyons on the soles of his clown-size ankle boots. He'll be off to the Lang girl's place now, where the Langs are never around. "Be careful, Josh." This is what I'd be telling him if I were a good mother. But consider these scars. This one here, for instance, from the diving rocks at the cottage when I was a kid. This one from a skate blade, this one from the back of my first lover's fist. And this one from the surgeon's knife where he went in after Josh—Josh, who wouldn't exist at all if his mother weren't so reckless.

"Sorry I didn't finish up the dinner stuff, Mom," he says. "But I gotta go." He gives me a stubbly peck on the cheek as he breezes by.

He'll make it, my boy will make it. He has no choice. Necessity, as they.... Oh yeah, and the Mothers of Invention. Frank Zappa, *Zoot Allures*. I played that album half to death. I can still conjure the jacket image if I close my eyes, the four long-hairs lounging against a wall, giving nothing away with those who-you-lookin'-at eyes.

> *Flies all green 'n' buzzin' in his dungeon of despair*
> *Who are all those people that he's locked away down there?*
> *Are they crazy? Are they sainted?*
> *Are they zeroes someone painted?*

I call out, "Be careful, Josh," just as the front door thumps shut. I go to the window in the living room, as I've done since he was yea high, and I watch him out of sight. That choppy stride, weirdly graceful, the occasional hop to keep from breaking my back. He's an accident, a perfect accident.

"You listen to me, young man," I say as he takes the corner.

sWeet chariot

T

"Now everybody—"

I looked over Jordan, and what did I see?
Coming for to carry me home . . .

White-haired, waggle-chinned men and women all around me are singing along, or at least lip-synching to this melancholy chestnut, fanning themselves with their lyric sheets. Most of them are smiling—grinning, even—as are the sons and daughters, the grandsons and granddaughters who've joined them on this field trip. My mother, too, attempts to smile. No go. She looks as though she's drowning, actually, and can't fathom why none of us will reach out and pull her to shore.

The woman leading the sing-along—she's introduced herself to us as Diana—has stepped down from the park's little stage onto the grass so she can stroll, strumming, amongst her audience. She's in her late thirties, I'd say, five years my junior. She wears her dark hair long and straight, the way girls wore it in the coffee houses way back when old folk songs were the new thing. She's even donned a peasant blouse of sorts, off-white with pale blue paisley against her Coppertone skin. There's a beaded band around her bronzed ankle—where the slave's shackle would have fit, I suppose. When she tips her warm gaze my way I make sure to be mouthing the words.

> *. . . A band of angels coming after me,*
> *Coming for to carry me home.*

She smiles at me, I smile back. I try to picture my mother with electrodes pasted to her head, Jack Nicholson in *One Flew Over the Cuckoo's Nest*, or Boris Karloff on Dr. Frankenstein's slab. I try to picture this in a good way, though, a happy way. I try to picture this as a healing experience for her.

Mom doesn't care, of course. If she cared we wouldn't be thinking of electrocuting her in the first place, my siblings and I. Mom doesn't believe the treatment will help, she believes it's a waste of time, like all the other treatments, the drugs, the dredging up of all those dreadful memories (which I've been spared, thankfully, but which must feature my late, my not-so-faithful father). Mom has no reason to submit to this new indignity—but then again she has no reason not to submit to it, either. She has no reason to do anything at all, one way or the other. Yet her heart keeps beating, her whole body persists in the foofaraw of living, a grim party grinding on long after everyone wishes they were home.

> *The brightest day that I can say,*
> *Coming for to carry me home . . .*

When I was a child my mother would often sing me to sleep, "Embraceable You," "I Cover the Waterfront," standards I still hear as lullabies. When the time came she did the same for my kids, first Rita, then Ray. She had a mesmerizing voice, a slightly gritty contralto. Up until two years ago you'd still hear it every once in a while, out in the kitchen while she fixed her trademark beef bourguignon, or in the garden while she deadheaded our geraniums.

Nowadays the kids will ask, "What's wrong with Nana? She doesn't sing any more, she doesn't even talk."

But she does, actually. Now and then, when we're alone, Mom will fight through all the layers of torpor and shame to ask me if there isn't some way I could just end it for her. Faced with my silence she subsides into an irritable muttering about the food, the staff, about Mrs. Essick, the moaner next door. The odd time my wife comes along for a visit Mom will make a foray into actual conversation. "Isn't that nice," she'll say. "How interesting."

It's nothing new. Way back in Christ's day they cured people with electric fish. The biggest side effect is that memories may be lost, in fact the last couple of years may be obliterated. Hallelujah.

. . . When Jesus washed my sins away,
Coming for to carry me home.

There's a brief smattering of applause, and wheelchairs are suddenly being steered back towards the waiting vehicles. My mother still walks—I take her arm, warn her to watch for sticks and roots underfoot.

I ask, "Did you enjoy the singing, Mother?"

"Lovely."

When the shuttle buses have left I turn, ready to start my walk back to the office. Diana is still packing up her things on stage. I wander over.

I say, "Can I help you with any of that stuff?"

"Oh, sure," she says. "Thanks. I'm just over there." I carry the chair and the music stand, she carries the guitar.

"You have a beautiful voice," I say, as she loads these things into the back seat of her car—a yellow VW bug, circa seventy-some-odd. I'm looking for flower decals.

"Thanks," she says. "I hope your mother liked it."

"I know she did," I say. "It's so important for them to get out. And music, well, it's the universal language, isn't it? Listen, can I buy you a cup of coffee? To express my thanks?"

"Oh, I don't know," she says. Then, "Why not?"

I open her door, grasp her bare elbow as she slides in. A little jolt of something passes between us, out of her body and into mine.

takeouT

T

Tweezing a choice bit of bamboo shoot from the stir-fry, Wendy says, "Would you still love me if you didn't know me?"

"What do you mean?" says Dick. "What are you talking about?" He grimly grips his chopsticks, scoops up a clod of rice and ferries it half way to his mouth before dumping it in his lap.

"I saw a show today," says Wendy. "On TV." Wendy sees a lot of shows on TV these days, and reads a lot of books. Officially, she's between jobs. Between friends (who never see her any more) it's understood that Wendy's suffered some sort of emotional breakdown, that she's refusing to seek help or join a support group, but that Dick—her husband of three years—is being wonderful about it anyway. A treasure.

"It was about people who'd been hit on the head," says Wendy, running a hand through her straggle of auburn hair. "Hard. People who went into comas and then came back, but couldn't remember three or four or five years of their lives. They'd look at their husbands or wives and say, you know, 'Who are *you*?'"

"Forget this," says Dick. He sets aside his chopsticks—the wooden kind that come in a single piece with takeout orders, and need to be snapped like a wishbone—and picks up his fork.

"Some of them," says Wendy, poking at a baby corncob at the bottom of a white cardboard box, "some of them are sticking together. They're keeping their vows. Some of them are separating because one of them isn't the same any more, isn't actually the person who took the vow."

"I wonder if you should maybe start doing stuff a bit," says Dick. "You know, just going out for a coffee or something with somebody every once in a while."

Wendy says, "Which kind would we be?"

"Pardon?" says Dick.

"If one of us were *different*, which kind of couple would we be? The kind of couple that stays together or the kind of couple that breaks up?"

"You tell me," says Dick. Then, on second thought, "The kind of couple that stays together."

"Because the thing is, Dick, I am different."

"Naw," says Dick, shaking his head. "Naw, you're still my Wendykins."

"Actually no," says Wendy. "No, I'm not your Wendykins. I'm Chiyono, a medieval Buddhist nun."

Dick looks up abruptly from the wreckage of his dinner.

"I've just achieved enlightenment," says his wife. "Just now, just today. I've been studying under Bukko of Engaku for quite a while. Sorry I didn't mention it—I didn't want to worry you. This afternoon I finally tore through the veil of illusion. I'm working on a little poem about it—would you like to hear it?"

"Um, yeah," says Dick. "Yeah, sure. Of course."

"It's no big deal," she says. She makes a series of incomprehensible noises—throaty, almost nasal, like the Orientals he's overheard in the cafeteria at work. “Oh, sorry,” she says, giggling. “Here.

> *At last the bottom fell out.*
> *No more water in the pail.*
> *No more moon in the water.*”

She shrugs, smiles shyly. “Do you like it?”

“Chiyono,” he says, slowly. “Chi-yo-no,” rolling the sounds between his tongue and palate, three little berries fit to burst.

cOtton

T

I still have the note she sent me, squirreled away in the Beefeater box with all my old class photos, report cards, honourable mentions. And I still remember the day Janet Something-or-other—started with a T—passed it on to me while Ms. Murray, our science teacher, was busy at the chalkboard. Water cycle, food chain.

The desire of each thing, the note read, and still reads—choppy blue script on a scrap of pink paper—*is to keep being what it is. The leopard hides so it can keep being a leopard, the leopard leaps so it can keep being a leopard, the leopard kills so it can keep being a leopard. But for creatures like us, creatures like you and me, this desire turns into a question and the question is, what am I? What should I do so I can keep being what I am when what I am is a question, what am I? Barb.*

Hm. Well, I wasn't quite sure how to take this message, but then again I wasn't quite sure how to take anything Barb ever did or said. This must have been the turn-on for me—being sucked out into the deep end, way over my head. It was no turn-on for most of the boys, who steered clear of her, too nervous even to tease. They went after the kinds of girls I too would be going after before long, girls who were easier to fathom, easier to impress. Feet on the bottom.

Tate, that was it, Janet Tate.

My message to Barb that day, as best I can recall, had gone something like this: *Barb, what are you doing after school?* Judging by her reply she'd read quite a bit more into these words than I'd intended. I decided my best bet was to toss a conspiratorial nod her way, as if to suggest I knew exactly what she meant, and couldn't wait to take it further.

I got this chance soon enough—before Ms. Murray made it to the bottom of the chalkboard the bell rang and we all gaggled out into the hall. Barb wandered by my locker, alone. Barb was always alone. She was tall, towering over me so that when I looked at her level I was gazing into the pale cup at the base of her throat. "Walk me home?" she said.

We took the long way, through the ravine alongside the "creek," an exposed storm sewer. I kicked rocks, threw pinecones. Barb talked. I can't remember, or even begin to imagine, what she said. At a certain point she simply stepped off the path, and I followed her.

In that same Beefeater box I have the project I handed in the following week. "Eli Whitney (1765-1825), Inventor of the Cotton Gin," complete with inept illustrations in coloured pencil and a little swatch of old pajama. My choice of subject had nothing to do with the fact that Thomas Edison and Benjamin Franklin had already been picked.

Cotton, I wrote, *is derived from the seed-hair fibre of a variety of plants of the genus Gossypium, native to most subtropical countries. The shrubby plant produces a creamy-white flower which soon turns deep pink and falls off, leaving the cotton boll containing the seeds. Seed hairs growing from the outer skin of the seeds become tightly packed within the boll, which bursts open upon maturity.*

It was a love poem, the only one I've ever composed, and I read it aloud in front of the whole class. Got an A+. I'm not sure Barb received it—she'd gone off me by then—but I had the moment. I have it still. That creamy white cotton against the deep pink where the elastic bit into her thigh. The brush of it, soft and warm as a leopard's belly, against my face. The rich rooty scent, as though the soil itself were rising up through her limbs.

I came close to showing these bits of memorabilia to my wife the other day, when I unearthed them (kids gone now, time to start culling our stuff, think about downsizing). I changed my mind. I have no idea where Barb is now, what happened to her—I heard at one point she'd gone strange, or stranger—but I know she was only half right. Sure, there's the desire to hang onto all this, to keep being what I am, even though what I am can only ever be a question—and a sorrow, I suppose, since what I am is always slipping away. But this desire has a sister, a twin, the desire to burst, to be absolutely and irrevocably transformed. This was the desire I knelt before that day, oozy earth beneath my knees, an odd young woman's fingers tangled up in my hair. "Let me out," I murmured, pressing my lips to the furrow in that fabric, the silent, topsy-turvy mouth withholding its mystery. "Let me in."

Ya Ya Ya

My daughter, Germaine, wanders out on stage with the other three members of her girl group. She looks great tonight, the usual walking corpse effect but with extra touches, bits of glinting machinery—springs, sprockets—caught up in the tangle of her turquoise hair. Her mom tisks beside me. They've never seen eye-to-eye on wardrobe.

Germaine straps on her guitar, plugs in. She slouches sweetly up to the mic. "How the fuck are ya?"

Hoots and whistles from the bar crowd, an alloy of first-year college kids and working stiffs.

"Whatever," says Germaine. "We're the Blades."

My wife elbows me. "Told ya," she says.

Germaine came by our condo late last night in a quandary over what she and the other "girls" (one of them's actually a guy waiting for his last sex-change operation) should call themselves. My vote was for the Boars, which I thought would play nicely to adolescent ennui, while symbolizing mythologically the dark, in a sense hermaphroditic aspect of the goddess and the sexual wound she inflicts. Betty backed up the Blades, though, for its bald allusion to castration anxiety, and more broadly to the themes of loss and separation that crop up so often in Germaine's lyrics.

This means I owe Betty a beer.

"This first song," Germaine says into the mic, which screams with feedback. She backs off a moment, approaches more cautiously. "This first song is called 'All That Is Perfect Wants To Die.' Sure, I stole it from Nietzsche. So sue me." And she bangs out the opening chord.

I'm thinking, has the girl got *style?*

Her mom leans up against me, beams proudly at the stage. Twenty years ago she was the one doing the screaming, while I stood by looking cool. Everything's coming together for us, here, now. Another perfect moment, dying.

I shout in her ear, "Wanna dance, beautiful?" First words I ever spoke to her.

"Ya, ya, ya," she howls. She loves me.

cOnviction

T

Ken slumps into a seat about halfway down the bus, weary after a long day's work. Well, not "work," exactly—Ken's currently unemployed. "Currently" isn't quite right either, "currently" makes it sound as though this is an unusual predicament for Ken, as though he's briefly and unavoidably between jobs, whereas in fact he hasn't bothered looking for work in months, and has never been hired to do anything fancier than scrub pots, sweep floors. Still, he's beat. He walked all the way downtown this morning to save on bus fare, and spent the day strolling the streets striving not to think about anything, about himself or the odd, terrifying world into which he was mysteriously extruded twenty-five years ago. About Sheri, for instance, the woman who most recently ditched him, or about Officer Jenkins, the neanderthal who chased him out of her building the other night, threatening to charge him with mischief...

On the seat beside him Ken notices a pink pamphlet entitled *Nine Things You Know When You're a Bahá'í*. He looks out the bus window. An elderly woman peers at her reflection in a compact mirror, touches her hair. A middle-aged man removes a cell phone from his sports jacket, begins speaking into it, bangs it against his palm, begins speaking into it again. Nine things? Might it really be possible to know nine things? Ken picks up the pamphlet.

1. You are a member of a single human family which includes every race, religion, nation and gender.

Ken permits himself a derisive little snigger over this gem. Almost immediately, though, he regrets it—as, indeed, he regrets almost everything he's ever done. After all, why shouldn't it be true, this idea that we're all just one big family? Certainly we fight the way families do . . .

Ken decides to move on, return to this first item once he has the hang of knowing things.

2. God loves all of us regardless of the time or place we live. That's why there have been many different prophets throughout history, each teaching humanity what it needed to know at a given time.

Now this, *this* is a proposition Ken's willing to get behind. Not the first bit, the bit about God loving us all—he'll need some time on that one. But the different-prophets-for-different-eras business—this makes sense to Ken. If there's any such thing as truth, Ken figures, it must be something that changes, something that matures or ripens or rots. Evolves, maybe, yeah, evolves. Why not? It stands to reason, then, that you'd need a new prophet to pop up every once in a while and offer an update. Ken's even willing to consider that he himself might be such a prophet. A prophet's just a person who isn't anything else—such, at least, is Ken's theory. A prophet's nothing at all, until he suddenly turns out to be a prophet.

3. You are responsible for your own spiritual growth, so you can't . . .

Sentences that begin in this way, sentences that come right out and advertise how skull-crushingly dull they're going to be, don't deserve reading. So Ken doesn't read it. He has his principles.

4. Women and men are equal. When we truly understand . . .

"Oh, sorry." A young woman sits down next to Ken, jostling him as she settles.

"That's okay," says Ken. He restrains himself from swiveling to peer at her, making do with little sideways glances. A brown, pudgy arm, tips of frizzy black hair brushing the startling convexity of a breast.

"Bahá'í," she says.

"Bye," says Ken. "Oh, I'm sorry, right. Bahá'í."

The woman laughs—guffaws, really. He sneaks that peek at her face. Round, rather pretty.

"I'm nothing," she says. "I mean, I was born Baptist, but I've never really believed any of it."

Ken nods. "I was like that too."

"Really?"

"Sure. I was born Methodist. I don't even know what that means, Methodist. But when I found this"—he waves the pamphlet, brandishes it almost—"it just sounded *right* somehow. Everything suddenly fit. You know?"

"I guess so," says the woman.

"Let me give you an example," says Ken. "What's your name?"

"Leona."

"Leona. Hi. I'm Ken."

"Hi, Ken."

"Okay," says Ken, "number five. *You are essentially good, but you must use your free will to develop your God-given potential.*"

"Essentially good?" says Leona. "I'm essentially good?" Her face does a long slow crumple—and she's crying.

Ken sits there for a time, stunned. He looks out the window, observes that the bus is just passing his stop. His house—his parents' house, technically, it's been ages since he's had his own place—is briefly visible up the street, a biggish bungalow with a sprinkler doing a stately tick-tock on its front lawn.

At the next stop Leona stands, starts for the door, still sniffling. She turns. "I feel like an idiot," she says.

"No," says Ken. "I mean, don't."

Leona shrugs. "I guess Bahá'ís only hang out with, like, other Bahá'ís, right?" She swabs her eyes with the sleeve of her T-shirt. "It's that kind of thing?"

"Yeah, I'm afraid so," says Ken. "Here, take this." He half rises from his seat, hands her the pamphlet. "There really is something for you to hold onto, you know. If you'd only reach out."

Leona smiles gamely. "Thanks. Maybe . . . I don't know."

"You never know," says Ken.

"You never know," says Leona, and steps off the bus.

Ken watches her disappear up a back lane as the bus pulls away. He looks down at his hand, his right, pamphlet-wielding hand, carefully examining the chaos of creases on his palm. "You will live a long, pointless life," he says. "You will have many chances, and you'll let them all slip away." But he doesn't say it with much faith, somehow, much conviction.

hiGh

T

"It's like Adam," said Adam, a great plume of sweet smoke erupting from between his lips. He passed me back the joint, one of his fat sloppy jobs now halfway gone. "Not me Adam, *the* Adam." He giggled—for such a big oaf Adam had an incredibly giddy, high-pitched laugh. "Madam," the other guys in residence called him behind his back. So did I, actually. It was a deadly bit of kidding, but at the time who knew?

"Yeah, I guess so," I said. Then, on further consideration, "What the hell are you talking about?" I inhaled deeply, returned the joint to him. Our thumb and fingertips made little puckering mouths, lightly kissed.

"Did he really fall?" said Adam. "I mean when he *fell* did he really *fall*?"

By way of reply I emitted a couple of those graphic clucking noises you make when you're fighting your body's urge to exhale.

"Tree of knowledge," said Adam. "Fruit." He giggled again.

"But what about my question?" I coughed, slumping back on my bed. "I asked you a question, didn't I?" Adam appeared all at once to be cut out extra crisply from his background—his own bed piled high with literature and philosophy books, and above it his prized William Blake poster, "Adam Naming the Beasts." In the poster a fey, curly-headed hunk caressed the snout of a serpent, while all the other creatures, all the nameable creatures filed by behind him. Lions, lambs. Six months into the school year and I was sick of it. "My question, help me out here. What was my question?"

"If we found you dead—" said Adam.

"Right, that was it. If you found me dead, if you found me pancaked on the front steps of the library like they found that grad student the other day . . ."

"Would we assume you'd fallen or—"

"Or I'd jumped," I said. "That was it. If you found me pancaked on the front steps of the library, would you assume I'd fallen or I'd jumped? Am I the kind of guy who falls off the top of a tall building or the kind of guy who jumps off the top of a tall building? That was my question."

"And my answer was, it's just like Adam," said Adam. "It's called the fall, but did he really *fall* when he fell or did he *jump*?"

This was the very question we'd one day be asking about Adam himself, of course, our Adam—two years later, I guess it was—but at the time who knew?

"Tree of knowledge," said Adam. "What did he know? After he fell what did he know that he didn't know before he fell?"

I reached over to receive the joint, sucked hard on the soggy stub.

"He knew he'd fallen," said Adam. "That's what he knew, that's the knowledge he gained from the tree of knowledge, from falling. The knowledge that he'd fallen." Adam was always coming up with crazy shit like this, mind-benders that bored me when I was straight but gave me an extra buzz when I was already high. That's why I was willing to smoke up with the guy, when nobody else would. Plus the fact that he was a pretty good roommate. Excellent stereo, excellent sense of when to get lost.

"Anyway," I said, "I guess Carla's going to be dropping by pretty quick."

Adam hesitated. This is what I remember most about that day, the beat he took before he went away. The rest of this memory I've probably cooked up—we can't really have been so prescient, can we, so precise in our foreshadowing?—but about the pause I'm certain. I have the sense it was some kind of pivotal moment for him, that there was something he was waiting for me to say.

Then he got up. "*Man* I've got a munch on," he said, heading for the door. "Time to eat." And he was gone.

Carla didn't show up for quite a while so I just lay there, already half hard, my head full of images and insights that would be lost to me when I came down.

passWord

Mackey, I type in—my mother's maiden name. This is what I've always used at the bank. But no.

Buster? The nickname my brother gave me as a kid, when I first started filling out. *Nipigon*? My home town. *Piaf*? The toy poodle I got for my tenth birthday, forty years ago now. No, no, no. "Incorrect password. Access to this file is denied."

Did I say forty years? Mary, Mother of God.

Well. The hot flashes I was expecting, the martyr-in-the-stew-pot feeling, the lighthouse-beacon earlobes, the extra ice cube in the martini, which still melts instantly in the cauldron of my palm. Yes, and the yo-yoing moods, the anxiety, the fatigue. But nobody warned me about the memory, the loss of memory. Or if they did (tee hee) it's slipped my mind.

Cassatt. Favourite painter. There's been a print of "Little Girl in a Blue Armchair" in Rae's bedroom for sixteen years now, a christening gift, a welcome-to-the-world gift from her grandmother, my mother. *Wordsworth.* Favourite poet.

> *Not in entire forgetfulness,*
> *And not in utter nakedness,*
> *But trailing clouds of glory do we come*
> *From God, who is our home. . . .*

Grade 12 English with Mr. Thomas—my decision to become a writer. Another little item that slipped my mind, another aspiration overlooked. So what have I been doing all this time? Or *Nin*, my favourite novelist, especially the sexy bits, written on commission at a buck a page for some lecherous booklover who insisted she cut out the poetry. She was my inspiration for writing the thing in the first place. Yes, *Nin*, surely. Or *Anaïs*. But no.

Two months later and it's what, just gone?

Hestia. Favourite deity, goddess of the hearth. *Catherine.* Favourite saint, who drank blood and pus to be at one with the afflicted. *Pooh.* Favourite character, or Rae's anyway, for all those years she couldn't sleep. No, no, no. I wonder how many of these computers come to grief on an average day here in the new millennium? Bludgeoned, battered with ergonomically perfected chairs, hurled from fifth-floor balconies? It's me, for Christ's sake. Though to be fair, I don't seem to be able to prove it.

Me? Didn't think so.

Perhaps I gave the thing a title and used that as the password. *Dream*? That's what it was, certainly, a dream, my reconstruction of a dream. In the dream it was Ronan, my husband, but in the written version I made it a stranger. I figured a stranger might better evoke the frisson of adventure I'd actually felt, dreaming about my husband. Or at least I think I made it a stranger, I'm pretty sure. *Reawakening*? *Reaffirmation*? Because that's what it felt like. But no, no, no. And each time that infuriating little "ting," like the car tisking at me for leaving on my lights.

This is the only file I've ever protected in this way. Is it my only secret? "Mom.doc"—as innocuous a file name as I could come up with, I suppose. What if Ronan ever comes prying, tries to open it, rattles at this locked drawer? Or Rae? What if they already have? What will they have guessed? What would they expect a middle-aged mother to hide?

On his way out the door this morning Ronan gave me a quick smooch on the lips and said, "Let's stay in tonight." As though we're always going out.

Or maybe I was being clever that day. Self-referential. *Password*, I type in, and I hold my breath. Ting.

Lick. Suck. Thrust. Sure, I resorted to the standard lusty lexicon, made do with the standard sexual gymnastics, but it all felt fresh that day, immersed as I still was in the dream, in the density of that wordless tryst. *Gasp. Sigh. Moan . . .*

It's still here, it's in me, I can prove it.

magdAlene

"You son of a bitch," says Cathy, sudsy hands on the edge of the kitchen sink. Bracing herself.

"Cathy, calm down," says Bill. He picks up a wine glass and begins carefully drying it. They'd used the good crystal with dinner even though they were alone, what the heck.

"You're worse than my father," she says. "At least he had the decency to screw around with his *own* secretary."

"Times change, honey," he says. "Think about it. I'll bet your mom never even had a secretary."

Cathy turns, stares at him. Soundlessly she opens and closes her mouth.

"Okay, not funny," he says. "I admit it. Hell, I've admitted this whole thing, give me credit for that at least."

"Oh, I do," she says. "I do. I admire you deeply, Bill, for your openness and your honesty. Confessing to having boffed my assistant—that can't have been easy. You have my most profound respect."

"Sarcasm is the lowest form of humour," he says.

"Go to hell." She reaches into the sink, draws out the little china pot they used for the chutney. She smashes it on the edge of the counter.

"Ouch," he says.

She examines her hands.

"You okay?" he says.

She nods, shakes her head, nods. "Super."

"If only I could explain it," he says. "This thing with Mary? It's different." He sets the glass carefully into the cupboard.

She says, "*Different*? What the hell's that supposed to mean?"

"I'll tell you. When I was a kid my sister had this painting in her—"

"Bill—" says Cathy.

"Cathy," says Bill, "just *listen* for a minute, will you?"

She raises her hands, still soapy, and lets them flap back down against her sides—a penguin resigning itself to flightlessness.

"Okay," says Bill. "So, my sister had this painting in her bedroom, or this print of a painting. My mother bought it as a souvenir from an art show that came through town. Old masters, it was a big deal. We all went. I don't remember the show except that I got incredibly bored and my penny loafers pinched and my mother kept saying 'divine.' She used to say 'divine' a lot, when she meant 'beautiful.'"

"She still does, Bill," says Cathy. "She still says that. Jesus."

"There you go," says Bill. "Anyway, what I do remember is that picture. I used to sit at the foot of my sister's bed a lot, while she was under the covers, and we'd talk about stuff. A lot of the time I wasn't looking at her, I was looking at that picture hanging over the bedside table. I had no clue at the time but it was by a guy named Luini, sixteenth century. Influenced by Leonardo, but sweeter and more devout by nature, Luini employed a soft chiaroscuro which allowed his colours almost to scintillate on the canvas. I looked him up."

"No shit," says Cathy. She opens the broom cupboard, takes out the broom and begins sweeping up the shattered pot.

"The woman in the painting was Mary Magdalene," says Bill. "Again, I didn't know that. She was just this woman, this odd young woman staring out at me all the time with these big swoony eyes. A little mouth, almost smiling. Curly red hair."

"Oh, please," says Cathy. She quits sweeping.

"And she's holding this little pot," says Bill, "and she's just lifting off the lid, delicately, with her thumb and her first finger. She's looking you in the eye, but she knows you're preoccupied with the pot, what could be in the pot."

"Mary," says Cathy. "Red hair."

"Cathy, it's *her.* That painting is *her.*"

"Let me get this straight," says Cathy. "You went after my assistant because she reminded you of a whore in a rotten old painting?"

"But Magdalene was no whore," says Bill. "That's the whole point. It's a complete myth. She was Christ's favourite disciple, she was the one he appeared to when he, you know, rose from the dead. I looked this up too. Nowhere does it say she was a whore. She had *seven demons* is what it says, but what does that mean? She probably had psychological problems. Depression, maybe, or anxiety attacks."

"*Anxiety attacks*?"

"Whatever. Anyway, what about all the men Christ exorcised? Does anybody assume they were whores?"

"You're so bloody enlightened, Bill. It slays me."

"What I'm saying," says Bill, "is that this thing with Mary was *meant to be* in some way. Destined."

"You know what, Bill?" says Cathy. "You need help. You need some serious help."

"Yes," says Bill. "*Yes.*"

cRunch

T

"What does it mean, in-fin-ite-ly small, Simon?" says my son. Stepson, really, which explains the first-name basis. We're side by side in front of the den computer in the standard attitude of supplication—a pair of cats peering hopefully into a hot-air vent—Barry in his PJs, me in the rumpled remains of my workaday suit. "How small is in-fin-ite-ly small?"

"Go ask your mother," I tell him. "Sorry, just kidding." But he kicks me anyway, with his little slippered foot.

For one thing, Barry's supposed to be flossed and brushed and in bed already. For another, this is supposed to be a project on basic astronomy, rings of Saturn, moons of Jupiter. Barry's tackled the origin of the universe. Ambitious little creature, takes after his mom, who's downstairs in her office right now clinching a deal with somebody on the far side of the earth, where the sun's already up again.

After a few false starts and some amusing detours—including an illustrated primer on the origin of the Miss Universe pageant (Long Beach, 1952, won by Finland's lovely Armi Kuusela)—we've found a website explaining that the universe was born ten or fifteen billion years ago in an event known as the Big Bang. At that time everything—and I mean *everything*, all matter, space and time—was scrunched up in an infinitely small, infinitely hot, infinitely dense little morsel, which blew up. Now, today, we're all still hurtling outwards from that initial blast, whizzing through space like chunks of cosmic shrapnel. So the story goes.

Working by tens up from zero, Barry and I have mastered the idea of a billion. A billion's nothing to us now, a billion's a breeze. Infinity, though, is turning out to be a trickier bit of business. Infinity isn't a concept I run into very often, myself, in my work with the government. Billion-dollar debts are routine for us, trillion-dollar debts, but what would an infinite debt look like, exactly?

"Tomorrow night," I tell him. "We'll work on infinity tomorrow night."

He kicks me again. Should I be doing something about this?

I tell him, "No matter how many times you kick me, you haven't kicked me an infinite number of times."

"Even if I kick you a billion times?"

"Even if you kick me a billion billion times. What's the biggest number you can think of?"

He says, "A billion billion billion billion billion billion billion billion billion jillion gazillion."

"That's nothing," I say. "Infinity's bigger than that, infinity's way bigger."

"Then how can something be in-fin-ite-ly small?"

Hm. "Well, I guess you'd just turn around and go the other way. What's the smallest thing in the world?"

"A cell," he says. "Wait, an atom." Little scholar. His dad's pretty quick, I gather, on the math-and-science side, engineer of some sort. Not that he deigns to share it much with his son, the sonofabitch. Maybe a weekend a month, maybe not.

"Okay," I say, "so you cut that atom in half, and then you cut it in half again. You cut it in half a billion billion billion billion billion billion billion jillion gazillion times. You keep on cutting it in half like that forever, and then you've got something infinitely small."

He says, "Forever?"

But my mind has begun to wander. While Barry was copying out the details of the Big Bang just now, I skipped on down the page to something called the Big Crunch. Nowadays, sure, the universe is still expanding, ballooning outwards with the energy of that first creative huff. It'll probably run out of steam one day, though, and start clutching at itself, sucking itself back in. Once it begins to collapse it won't stop until it's all packed into that single dot again—infinitely small, infinitely hot, infinitely dense.

What interests me is the point smack dab in the middle. What interests me is the moment at which the whole thing quits expanding but hasn't yet begun to contract. The moment of stillness—between swelling and shrinking, systole and diastole—when the world stops being born and starts dying. Will we feel it? Will we know?

"Hey, can anybody in here tell time?" Barry's mom looms in the doorway, fists on hips, trying to look stern. What she really looks, though, is exhausted. Her thin face appears heavy, somehow, gravity-stricken. Her bun has come unraveled on one side, blond ringlets falling around her neck, stiffened here and there with grey. Her black skirt is unbuttoned at the side. If Barry weren't here I'd tug it down, take her onto my lap.

"I just have to figure out this one thing," says Barry.

I scoop him up, throw him over my shoulder. "Make it a quick one."

"If everything's *inside the little dot*," says Barry, squirming like a squirrel in a sack, "what's the little dot in?"

Would any real spawn of mine have been able to come up with

that question? What can I possibly say that will count as an answer?

"Never mind," says Barry. "I'll ask my dad."

But it's his mom and I who tuck him in, who make a Barry sandwich of him on his little blue bed, and it's to us he keeps saying, "Stay forever."

Brood

Here's one of my favourites. There's a knock at the front door one evening, a shy, tentative tapping—seductive, if that's possible, the sort of knock that makes you run a hand through your hair, check your fly on the way to the door. It's Ruby Morris from down the block, Ed's wife. She's all choked up about something. I place a hand on the small of her back—the delicate dip from which her rump so bravely rises—and steer her to the couch.

"You've just missed Tess, I'm afraid," I say. "She's gone out with the girls for the evening, probably be late."

"Stuck home with the kids, are you?" says Ruby.

"Actually, they're sleeping over at their Aunt Lucille's," I say. Or they're off at camp, whatever.

I hand Ruby a drink. She takes one long, shaky pull at it—and she pours out her heart. How she and Ed have been struggling for years, timing it to her cycle, saving it all up for just the right night. How she's had herself checked—"fertile as an alluvial fan," is how the doctor has described her.

"If Ed finds out he's the problem he'll just die," says Ruby. "It's so important to him to be, you know, a real man. I've got to do something." She looks at me, how would you put it . . . *imploringly*.

I say, "It's okay, I understand." I enclose her little hand in mine, lead her upstairs. I unbutton her, unzip her—and I take her. No synthetics, no goops or gizmos, no nothing (not that Tess and I bother with any of that gear any more either, now that she's had the operation). I explode deep within her, abandoning myself to the embrace of her ravenous womb. "Thank you," she cries into my mouth. "Thank you."

Then there's Tabitha, my secretary—whoops, executive assistant—a single woman who asks daily, dreamily after my kids, Carissa and Dean. We usually do it right there on my desk, sweeping aside the family photos in their gilt frames—but missionary position, of course, for maximum oomph fertility-wise. "He'll bear your name," she whispers.

Marie, my therapist—a whiz-kid on whom I've fathered quite the fantasy brood, believe me—claims she's seeing more and more of this all the time. There's no magazine dedicated to us yet—*Knock-Up*?—no website, no secret society. But just wait.

Marie has a theory about us, as she has about so many things. The old fetishes will fade, she believes, slowly expire of exposure, but this new one will flourish.

"Up until now perversity has meant unreproductive sex, barren sex," she says. "Oral, anal, auto, homo, phone. Cyber. Sadomasochistic. And of course just plain old protected. Perversity meant doing it for yourself, finding a way to foil mother nature, fool her into giving you the pleasure of orgasm without burdening you with the baby. The new you. The usurper." Like I say, brains up the whazoo.

But nowadays, of course, as Marie points out, mother nature herself is into bondage. She's shackled and gagged, taking it the hard way from about six billion of us every day, and counting. "At a time like this," says Marie, "what could be kinkier, what could be crueler than to reproduce?"

Did I tell you about Rose? Rose is the bald, tattooed bull dyke who comes clanking through my office once a week wearing a drawer-full of hardware and pushing a Hoover. Imagine we both work late one evening, and she invites me back to her loft for a nightcap. On the way she explains that she and her partner—Lee, let's say—are longing to have a baby. They've been looking for a father, but there's a complication. Seems Lee is a passionate girl—she's left cold by the turkey baster. The father, then, is going to have to . . . well, he'll be required to . . .

I say, "It's okay, I understand."

Lee—a real Venus of Willendorf type, hips and bosom primed for procreation—receives us at the door in a sweet, housewifey sort of way. She pours us drinks, and we sit around speculating about names. Lee leans towards Ella, Billie, Betty—the jazz divas. Rose would rather a historical figure of some kind, Joan, Marie.

"How about Cleo?" I say. "After Cleo Laine, short for Cleopatra? Goes both ways."

We all laugh. The women nod approvingly in my direction—they've picked the right man for the job.

Rose rises, then, pecks Lee and me on the cheek. "I could use a breath of fresh air," she says. "If there's any left."

In the bedroom—Lee and I alone—it's straight down to business. Nothing fancy, no leather, no leash. Lee's flesh itself is the only fetish. Warm, aromatic, almost alive.

vEssel

T

"Talk to me," he says, as though she needs reminding. "Oh wait, the pink pill."

"Here you go," she says. "Let me just . . . that's it. Comfy?"

"Uh-huh. Now talk to me. Please."

"Today I'll be exploring the uses of literature," she says. Her voice, still soft, has suddenly modulated in tone—she sounds as though she's addressing a great lecture hall full of bedridden old men now, rather than just this one. "Literature's useless, of course, that's why we love it, but if you're going to pursue it as a way of life you'll have to tell people *something* to keep them off your case . . . The kids gave me a little titter for that one today, my dear. Here, let me plump that up for you."

She lifts his head—bald as a baby's now, soft and cool as a peach in her palm—and rearranges his pillow. This is the same pillow she's so often tucked under her tush to intensify the pleasure of his thrusting.

"Thank you," he says. Still the gentleman. When he quits being courteous she'll know it's really over.

"I'm going to talk about two uses for literature," she intones, "one ethical, one spiritual. Somebody—ten marks if you know the source—once said that 'the great power of a good book is that it makes it harder to tell *us* from *them*.' This is the—"

"Excuse me, darling," he says. His eyes have cracked open again, two slits of glacial blue in the sickroom's yellow light. "I'm sorry, but did I have my red pill?"

"Yes, my dear," she says. "You had your red pill, you had everything you need."

"Thanks," he says.

"Of course, darling. Now where was I. Yes . . . No, I'll skip a bit. Literature . . . literature shows us other lives from the inside. Literature demonstrates that other people's worlds are every bit as compelling, every bit as rich and raw and . . ."

As she speaks she strokes her lover's wrist, the soft white spot where she'll someday search for his pulse. She's been through this with her father already, it's second nature. Twelve years ago, when she first fell in love with this man, her father was alive and well. Still, friends felt no compunction about analyzing her "father complex." It's always astounded her, the way people can be sure.

"If the ethical value of literature is that it makes other people real to us," she's saying, her voice softer now, "the spiritual value of literature is that it makes us unreal to ourselves. To borrow a couple of Richard Rorty's words, the ethical burden of literature is *solidarity*, but the spiritual burden of literature is *irony*. Literature shows us that character is created out of context, out of contingency. It leads us to understand that we too . . ."

Her voice gradually slows, in synch with the slowing of his breath. Each of his exhalations is deeper now, more abdominal. He's right on schedule—ten minutes into a lecture, most nights, and he's gone. In the morning he'll apologize, as he apologizes every morning. She'll assure him, as she assures him every morning, that he hung on longer than most of her kids.

"Literature shows us that while fictional characters are real," she's saying, "real people are fictional. Real people too are 'empty,' as the Buddhists say, devoid of self-nature. A person isn't a thing—things aren't things either, of course—but a space, a clearing in which the rest of the world can take place. Literature helps purge us of the whole idea of a 'self' or a 'soul,' the bizarre notion that there's some inviolable lump of goodness-knows-what at the core of us. Literature's the miracle cure for metaphysics, for the dream of absolute— Okay, honey, it's okay."

He's entered his twitching phase, his limbs working out all the little tensions accruing from a day of strained immobility. She places a hand on his chest, presses.

"Literature," she murmurs, "teaches us that words like 'body' and 'soul' aren't names for separate entities, for discrete chunks of ourselves, but simply sounds we make to shape our attention. Literature teaches us that words like 'I' and 'you' aren't hatchets to be used for hacking up the world, but—"

He's snoring, at last. His mouth has fallen open—an empty vessel which once held her name. She can faintly make out the pink moonscape of his palate. It brings to mind a poem.

time and spaCe

T

Six more hours until I see you again, two on the bus, two on the ferry, two more on the bus. A finite amount of time, both long and short—like life! (I'm feeling profound here, look out.) I'll have to ration my coffee. Rakel topped up the thermos for me before I left, preheating it with water from the kettle so my coffee wouldn't go cool on my way to you. I ought to have felt awful, but I didn't, I felt full, I felt sodden, I felt supersaturated with love. Perhaps this is what we all need, more love than we deserve. Love leeched, love coerced from the people around us through little acts of cruelty.

Six hours should be time enough to finish reading this book, or to achieve enlightenment, one or the other. I haven't decided. The book is called *Axel*, the imaginary diary of a failed composer who befriends a great composer. A creature with a voice, a creature with no voice. A stranger who cries out, a mute stranger, in the end what's the difference? (Am I being deep here, or just gloomy?) It's a black book, lies nicely open in my lap, but then there's enlightenment. Just think, if I were to achieve enlightenment at the very moment we pulled into the depot! I'd step off the bus, and there you'd be in your leather skirt and fuzzy white sweater (or your green jodhpurs and beige blouse, or your blue jeans and maroon pullover), and you'd take one look at me and know something was different, without knowing quite what. If enlightenment turned out to be something a person could tell about, I'd tell about it. Otherwise I'd keep quiet. We'd get something to eat, sushi, Shanghai noodles, whatever. We'd lose our appetites, and we'd rush back to your place.

Will it be different, when I'm enlightened? I hope so. I imagine everything the same, only a million times better, a billion times.

I learned an exercise, a spiritual exercise once on a retreat with Rakel. She knew this guru, pallid as I am but very advanced, apparently, very evolved. This is before I met you. Can you imagine that, a time before we met? Can you imagine a time before you were born? That's the exercise we did with our guru. *Imagine the world without you.* Very pleasant, in a peculiar sort of way.

Here's another one. It puts you in touch with the infinite. Okay, so you close your eyes. You look down, way down into the deep, dark space inside you. It's a well, a cavern, it's black, it's so much emptiness, all the emptiness in the world gathered in. And then I forget what you do.

civilizEd

What would I say if you ever actually answered the door? *Carpets need shampooing, Ma'am? Would you be willing to support the Save the Marmot fund? May I please have my husband back, please?*

I got your cleaning lady, once. Philippine, is she? "No-no, nobody," she said to me, waving her duster around to demonstrate just how empty the house was. She had a kerchief over her hair, a beautiful deep blue against that scrumptious brown skin. Perhaps I could borrow her sometime, when I'm throwing a dinner party. That's what civilized women do, you know, they borrow one another's cleaning ladies. "I don't suppose I could have Maria for Thursday?" they say. "I wouldn't ask, but I'm hosting my book club. We're doing, what's it called, where it's God talking through him? So *inspiring.*"

Another time I got one of your daughters. The older one, I forget her name. Your figure, your nose. Keith showed me a picture of you once, or at least he left it in a drawer where I had no trouble finding it. You're sitting on a rock by a river, looking off into the distance as though you're thinking something. Trying not to blink, I suppose. Keith claimed you weren't all that pretty, the time I asked, and he wasn't lying (that *is* quite the beak, my dear). But you're attractive in a big-boned, hyperbolic kind of way. I take out that picture sometimes, and try imagining I'm a man. I'm pretty sure I'd want to screw you too.

Your daughter told me, "My mom isn't home."

I said, "May I speak to your father, then?"

"He isn't my father," she said. "I mean, my father doesn't live here any more. There's nobody home."

"You shouldn't say that," I said to her. "You should say, 'Mom's in the shower,' or 'Dad'll be home any minute.' You haven't the faintest idea who I am." She looked stricken, poor girl, but it was for her own good. At that age they have no idea how vulnerable we all are, how easily we can be damaged.

Truth is, I only knock when I'm almost positive no one's around. If my husband ever answered, though, I know exactly what I'd do. I'd say, "Sir, do you believe in a perfect world? Have you taken Jesus into your heart?" I'd play it so straight he'd believe one of us had been touched. I'd convert that son of a bitch.

And if you appeared? I'm still not sure. Perhaps that's why I do it, to figure out what I have to say to you.

Here's a question I'd like to ask. I'd like to ask, do you love him for the same reason I love him? I don't see how you could. I love him for something he said long before he met you. You were with your own man, back then, and I was with mine.

It was the first time I brought Keith home to my folks. They were religious people, or at least my father was religious, and my mother never crossed him (ha). We sat down to dinner, the four of us, and my father said, "Keith, why don't you say grace?" It was a trap, of course, Keith never took the Lord's name *except* in vain, and Dad knew it. Scaring off boyfriends was my father's favourite, pretty much his only hobby.

"Dad," I said, "I don't think—"

"I'd love to," said Keith. Didn't miss a beat. He closed his eyes, took my hand. He said, "Thank you, God, for all this wonderful food. And thank you for letting me find this perfect woman." He meant what he was saying, too, meant every word of it. That was the miracle. And then he said, "Thank you, God, for blessing us with a child."

You could have flattened my father with your little finger, believe me. This was the nightmare that had haunted him since the day I was born. It was at that exact moment I realized something. I can't say just what I realized, but I can tell you it made all the difference to me. What was happening to me was my own life, my real life. The baby didn't work out, none of the babies worked out (don't worry, it was me, Keith'll knock you up just fine) but that moment was already perfect, irredeemable.

I want us to be civilized about this, I'd say to you. But there'd be something about the way I said it.

neW messages

T

In the corner of your computer's screen, this message: *You have new messages.* You stretch, check your watch. Maybe a bite of lunch.

You wander into the kitchen, pull the ruins of last night's pizza from the fridge—a perk of working at home. Feta, mushrooms, olives.

You take up your usual spot in the living room, plate in your lap, flip on the tube. In black and white, the old *Addams Family*, Gomez kissing Mortitia's marbled arm from wrist up to elbow, then back. "Mwa, mwa, mwa, mwa, mwa." The scene gives you an almost undetectable little rush of eros-tinged nostalgia.

You switch to the nonstop news channel. An anchorwoman you don't recognize—terrific cheekbones, Chiclet teeth—sits behind a desk looking earnest. "We have a call from a young man named Thomas," she says. "Thomas has dialed us on his cell phone from the school. Thomas, can you hear me?"

"I can hear you," says Thomas.

You gnaw your pizza, wish your new lover understood about anchovies.

The anchorwoman says, "Thomas, where are you right now?"

"I'm in my classroom," says Thomas. "I'm hiding."

"Where are your classmates?"

"They ran out."

"Why didn't you run with them?"

"They were being shot."

In the corner of your television screen, this message: *Breaking News—Armed youths occupy high school.*

The anchorwoman says, "You heard shots, Thomas?"

"Yeah."

"Can you hear anything now?"

"I can hear screaming," he says. "And crying. And shooting, every once in a while."

The anchorwoman says, "Can you see anything?"

"I can see you."

"Pardon me?"

"I can see you. I'm watching TV."

"You have a TV in your classroom, Thomas?"

"Yeah. Now I see the SWAT team."

The anchorwoman has disappeared from your screen, to be replaced by a phalanx of black, helmeted figures with guns. They sneak along the wall of a large brick building, stopping to consult now and then, and to confer with other people on walkie-talkies.

The anchorwoman says, "Do all the classrooms have televisions?"

You see where she's going with this. You picture the gunmen—gunboys—tuning in from somewhere else in the school. Cursing as their names are mispronounced.

"Yeah," says Thomas. "I mean, most classrooms do."

The anchorwoman says, "Thomas, I think you should hang up now, okay? Maybe call home?"

"Okay," says Thomas.

The phone beside you rings. You stare at it a moment, pick it up.

"Hello?"

"Hi Dad. Um, I forgot my soccer stuff."

"What?"

"I forgot my soccer stuff."

"Again?"

"I'm really sorry," he says. "Dad, this is a big game."

A view from the air now, a building-block complex ringed by police cars and armoured trucks.

"Your soccer things are your own responsibility," you say.

"I know that, Dad. I can't miss this one."

A suburban front lawn. Adolescent boys and girls sit dazed, or stretch out to be tended to by people in white uniforms. You push a button, change channels.

"These the quarter finals?" you say.

"Yeah. Northtown. We own them."

"...Okay, the usual spot."

You wait for his ecstatic "*Yes*," and then you hang up.

Mortitia and Gomez are mid-tango now, a long-stemmed rose in her teeth. The kids—Wednesday? Pugsley?—sit by contentedly tugging on one another's hair.

sunday morninG

T

"This is interesting," says Paul.

"Hmm," I say, keeping my eyes on my section of the newspaper. I'm halfway into an article about teenage girls in malls, straight-A girls in hundred-buck Nikes, how they're being recruited by pimps and drug pushers. Paul and I don't have kids yet, but it may not be long. I find myself tuning in to this kind of stuff all of a sudden. Faulty car seats. Child molesters. Date rape.

"Listen," he says, ignoring the fact that I'm ignoring him. "On death row? When they're killing somebody, administering the lethal injection?"

"Hmm."

"They have two executioners," he says. "They each have a button, and they push their buttons at exactly the same moment. One of the buttons delivers the toxin, the other's a dud."

"Hmm." I flick my eyes back and forth across my page, furrow my brow. Since Paul moved back in things have been much better than before, but I do miss my mornings.

"Don't you get it?" Paul persists. "Neither of them's guilty. Only one of them's done the killing, and nobody knows which one."

"Somebody must know," I say.

"Nobody knows."

"What about the person who set it up? Hooked up the buttons? That person knows." I sip my coffee, lean intently over the breakfast table. *Low self-esteem*, I read, *is another contributing factor.* Low self-esteem is a contributing factor in the case of pretty much all earthly evils, as far as I can tell. When our baby pops out I'm going to have Paul and a few friends on hand to give her a standing ovation.

"Not necessarily," he says. "Not necessarily. They could connect the buttons to a computer, a randomizer. Then no one knows."

"Except God," I say.

"Pardon me?"

"Except God." I'll finish with the pimps when Paul goes for his shower. I look up at him. There are lines on his cheek, a detailed diagram he's picked up from the pillow. "God knows."

"God?" He says it the way my grandma says "email."

"God would know," I say. "Unless there's no God. It's a paradox, actually."

"What is? What's a paradox?"

"One of them's the real executioner, right? The real murderer? Well, his only hope of salvation is that there's no God, no salvation. Then his secret's safe—even he doesn't know it. But if there's a God, he's damned."

Paul does a sort of double take here. Runs a hand through his goofy hair, gives me a look. "A woman gets pregnant," he says. "She's had two men, two lovers. Nobody knows for sure which one is the father."

"Paul," I say.

"The woman goes for an abortion," he says. "No blood test, so there's no way to know which guy's baby she's—"

"You son of a bitch," I say.

"I'm going for my shower," he says. He stands up, sort of staggers out of the room.

I look back down at my newspaper. There's an illustration, pen and ink. A young woman in high heels runs down a long corridor, glancing over her shoulder. She's going to twist an ankle, trip, you just know it.

the inVention of language

"You're still not getting it, Arthur," she says. "For us, for women, it's not just a matter of speaking out. There aren't even words for what we have to say. Language itself has to be reinvented."

They're sitting in the window of a deli in a strip mall, old friends, nibbling at croissants, staring out at the dismal geometry of parked cars. With her foot she rhythmically joggles a stroller. A faint, experimental cooing issues from beneath the heap of rumpled blankets.

"But Kiri, aren't we all struggling against that tyranny of words?" he says. He glances anxiously at the stroller, lowers his voice. "Against a verbal status quo? I mean, language always wants to keep on saying what it's always said. Each of us has to somehow subvert it, recreate it."

She says, "Yeah, but it's different, Arthur, it's not the same. Men made up this vocabulary, this syntax. It's yours." With an upturned palm—as if delivering it to him, waitress-style—she indicates the world outside the window, its trite, predictable symmetries, its squalid utilitarianism. "It's yours. You say what you want with it."

These words fill him with shame, and with a sickening, inarticulate rage. A sense of violation, helplessness—precise, yet inexpressible. He takes a deep breath, releases it. "How's little Marie?" he says.

Instantly, from beneath her muffle of covers, Marie begins to howl.

"Too long we've kept silent," says her mother. "Too long."

beyond stillneSs

T

We should be talking about big things, my father and I, intimate things, what's really on our minds. We're sitting on his back stoop looking out at his garden, still bountiful despite the drought, despite his illness. This is our first time together since the news turned really bad—it's three thousand miles, and I've been crazy busy. The noonday sun glares down at us with that know-it-all gaze from which you have no choice but to avert your eyes.

"I once threw up in your tomato patch," I say to him. No, I don't, but I ought to. This is what's really on my mind.

It was a sweaty August evening, the evening of a day just like this one, twenty-five years or so ago. My plan for that evening was to touch Grace Paul's breast. I'd already had my tongue in her mouth three times, touching her breast seemed like a perfectly sensible next step. Still, I was nervous I suppose, gulping a little too frantically from the plastic jug of Smirnoff's and Tang I'd brewed up for the occasion. We were leaning against one another in the darkness of this very garden, just over there by the garage. We were licking one another's lips, I was just easing my hand from her hip up her belly when the vodka got the better of me.

Grace took the puking thing kind of personally, I'm afraid. I never did get to touch her breast. I don't suppose I ever will, now. Who knows where Grace Paul is any more, if that's even her name? She might be Grace Gordon by now, or Grace Levinsky, she might have achieved enlightenment and be going by Grace Babaganesh for all I know. She and her breasts are eternally out of my reach. For some reason this strikes me, just today, as tragic.

"Tell me again about the light," says my father.

It should really be the other way around though, shouldn't it? Him telling me about stuff? What it was like for him when I was a kid, maybe, or even before that, when he and Mom were new lovers and I was nothing but potential, nothing but an ecstatic sort of dread down deep in their bones. Or later on when she left him, at a time when men and women didn't leave one another. Things no one else can possibly know.

"Tell me again about the light," says my father. Like a kid pleading for the same bedtime story night after night. A kid with a great plume of white hair and yellowing eyes.

I picture tumours burgeoning in his brain and his liver and his lungs—little clusters of cherry tomatoes. Secondary tumours, they're called, sprouting from seeds released by the skin cancer on the back of his neck. *Melanoma:* dark tumour. *Metastasis:* beyond stillness.

"For light, there's no such thing as time," I say to him. I learned this from an article I read on my flight here, in a science magazine I picked up at the airport. I read the article three or four times through, trying to comprehend it, trying to believe it. I told my father about it that first day, and he keeps begging for more. "For light, or for anything traveling at the speed of light,"

I say to him, "all distance is completely condensed. That means it takes no time to arrive. Anywhere. From our point of view it takes light, what is it, five minutes to get here from the sun? From the point of view of the light it takes *no time at all.* Zero."

My father shakes his head, grinning, incredulous. The way he used to grin when I'd report to him on some little accomplishment of mine, a nifty catch at first base, a passing grade in some subject he'd always flunked. Something that allowed him to live, for the moment, outside himself.

I say to him, "No matter where light's going, it's already there. It touches everything in the universe at once. *Now*, I guess you'd say. *Always.*"

"I've never seen the tomatoes look so good," my father says to me, still shaking his head. "You'll take some home for Carey and the kids?"

"Sure, of course," I say. "Hey, do you by any chance remember a girl named Grace Paul?"

"What, from the school orchestra? With the . . . ?" And he makes the universal sign for a well-favoured woman, hefting the air before his wasted chest. This is something my father wouldn't do. The doctors did mention that, with the brain thing, his inhibitions could soon be slipping away.

Good, this'll speed things up, there might still be time.

neither nOr

At the hospital you step into an elevator going up, unoccupied but for a charming if slightly haggard brownish man who puts you in mind of Nagarjuna, the second-century Buddhist whose point of view exhausted all points of view, left the morning perfectly free again, no appointments. Could it be him, could it be Nagarjuna? Could it be anybody else? Is there any point your holding an opinion on this issue one way or the other? Isn't the whole goal to transcend opinions, to cease discriminating between this and that, one thing and the next?

You push your button, top floor. He checks his watch, a gentle reminder of the essentially non-essential nature of things, of connectedness, contingency. Impermanence. Emptiness too is empty, of course, devoid of self-nature. It's him all right.

The question is whether or not to speak up. Perhaps he'd be pleased, appreciate being recognized for once, after all these years—hell, centuries. Or perhaps he'd prefer to be left to his own profound, his own ineffable (is that the word?) meditations. No way to know. All you can know is that in a moment this moment too will be gone, like all the other moments, sucked back to its dim origins in the warm squishy void where your other kidney used to be. Live a little.

"No being in things," you say, "no non-being in things. Neither either-or nor neither-nor." Nothing. You clear your throat. "Not being," you say. "Not non-being," you say. "Not not being, not not non-being," you say—showing off now. "Not—"

"Do I *know* you?" says the man, pivoting to face you. "I'm sorry, but do I *know* you?"

If there's no such thing as a self, after all, how can a self be known? Very good. Oh, it's him. You're as certain of this as you've ever been of anything. Which admittedly isn't all that—

Ping. The elevator doors part, Nagarjuna steps off. Cardiology. *Heart Sutra*, of course. *Form is exactly emptiness, emptiness exactly form* . . . The world's a kidder, the world's a card. Brings to mind something Meister Eckhart once said to you, the day you bumped into him on the Richardson bus, the #1. Or perhaps it was you reminding him of his own words. *Only he knows the divine who recognizes that all creatures are nothingness . . . If the soul is to know the divine it must forget itself and lose itself. . . .*

A woman joins you in the elevator, steps delicately aboard, a lovely sad-eyed lady from whom you avert your sad eyes. Mary, Mother of God. And up you go, together.

biaFra

T

"There are children starving to death in Biafra," Wendy's mother would often announce towards the end of dinner, meaning, "Finish up your meatloaf and peas." She'd deliver the line matter-of-factly, but with a slight, long-suffering weariness—eyebrows up, head tipped to one side—as though the children starving to death in Biafra were a personal tribulation of hers, a trial visited upon her by her own ungrateful kids. Grudgingly, Peter would shovel his last few forkfuls of food into his mouth, beg the car keys from his dad and slouch out of the house. Wendy too would scour her plate and then, with painstaking care, empty every serving dish of its scraps, a chicken leg, a fistful of pickles, a few dollops of mashed potato. When Wendy hit a hundred and ninety pounds her mother quit it with the starving Biafrans.

In her first year at college Wendy signed up for a course in political economy. Professor Beck, a young firebrand sighed over by many of the young women, led Wendy to understand that children were starving to death in places like Biafra—"which was reabsorbed into Nigeria many years ago, by the way," as he corrected her—not because ignorant, privileged brats like her ate too little, but because they ate too much, because they were consuming far more than their fair share of the world's finite resources. Halfway through her second serving of ratatouille at the campus cafeteria that night Wendy set down her fork. In the washroom she flushed the toilet again and again to drown out the sound of her retching. When Wendy hit a hundred and ten pounds her parents came to collect her, loading her trunk and her stereo into the back of their minivan.

Wendy loathed her therapy group until she got to know Alexandra, a young woman who'd just recently survived a similar episode. "Girl," Alexandra said to her confidentially after one session, "girl, you gotta get yourself strong. You wanna change the world, you gotta get yourself strong." The next day Wendy dyed her hair orange, the perfect complement to Alexandra's blue. The two went together to get pierced, first noses, then tongues, then belly buttons. Wendy scored a job washing dishes at the café where Alexandra worked the espresso machine. They rented an apartment, took turns cooking vegan meals, carrot loaf, polenta pie. They wrote letters to politicians, marched in rallies, chained themselves to buildings and machines. When Wendy was arrested for the third time her parents left her in jail overnight to think things through.

The guard who led Wendy to her cell assured her it had to be bad karma that kept getting her arrested, that her rotten luck was related to some nastiness she'd committed in a previous life. "Spend a few years in prison," said the woman, "like I have, and you'll learn something about karma." She further explained that Wendy must have been "pretty damn good" last time around, though, since she'd been born to well-heeled parents in a ritzy part of the world. "You end up where you ought to end up," she said, as she clanged shut the cell door. "You get what you deserve." When Wendy's parents came to collect her the next morning Wendy said to them, "I'm sorry," and gave them each a hug.

I represented her in court the next month, one of my very first cases. Dumb luck, I got her off with no prison time. We started dating, lived together for a couple of years, got pregnant, got married. Mark is eight, now, Rebecca is five, almost six. Each week we have them drop a few coins into a coffee tin on the kitchen counter. The proceeds go to a little girl named Nisha who lives in Nepal, and make it less likely, we're told, that Nisha will be sold into slavery. There's a picture of Nisha on our fridge, a grinning child with pigtails and huge, slightly crossed eyes, squatting at her mother's feet. Her mother wears a faded UCLA T-shirt, lime green.

Wendy will often slip this picture out from under its magnet ("Today is the first day of the rest of your life!") and set it on the table while she sips her coffee. The kids are relieved, as am I, when she puts it back.

rose-breasted grosbeaK

We're at home not panicking.

"We should have gone," says my wife. "Why on earth didn't we go?"

"Jeanie didn't want us to," I remind her, just as she reminded me three or four minutes ago. "Besides, Josh is a good man, he'll know what to do." I have my doubts that Josh is a good man, actually, but this doesn't seem the time to mention them. Last check-in call he said to me, "Jeanie's a real trooper." Trooper?

"Anyway, I was twenty-six hours with Jeanie," says my wife, not for the first time. She seems to have forgotten I was there.

Jeanie has been thirty-nine and a half hours so far. Thirty-nine hours and forty minutes. Our first call came at dinner time night before last, and we've just now finished straightening up today's breakfast things. It's Thursday but I'm not going in, to hell with it. One year from retirement, I can't take a morning off while my baby has a baby?

Narrow hips, is an expression that's been bandied about. Also *best for both mother and child.*

"Besides, we'd be ninety minutes getting there," I say. "Anything could happen." This had always been one of our concerns about moving to the country.

"There he is!" cries my wife. She's got her nose pressed up against the kitchen window.

"Where?" I say.

"The birch, look. Second branch—"

"I see him. Oh, you beauty. Grab the glasses."

She hands me our brand new Bushnell binoculars.

"Now read it to me again."

My wife flips through the field guide. "*Male has black head and back, rose red breast. White underparts, white wing bars, white rump.*"

"That's him," I say. "That's our baby."

"*Call is a sharp eek.*"

"Eek?"

"Eek."

We strain our ears. The phone rings—I bang my forehead with the binoculars.

"Hello?" says my wife into the receiver. Pause.

"Pardon?" says my wife. "I don't understand." Pause.

"Well?" I say.

There are all at once tears weaving their way down my wife's face, wrinkle to wrinkle. "Jesus," I say. "What is it? What?" She's just standing there, crying.

I grab the phone from her. "Hello?"

"Oh, hello, sir. Sir, are you concerned at all about the destruction of the old growth forests?"

"Hello?" I say, more loudly. "Who is this?"

"I'm with the Nature Conservancy, sir. Sir, perhaps you've heard about the ozone layer? You may not be aware, though, that the sun's rays are already—"

"What the hell's going on?" I shout, and I slam down the phone.

It rings again.

and yard out all my wisdom teeth. Typical Western way of dealing with pain, as Mitch says. But if the tooth—twisted, cramped, stymied—is just a metaphor or whatever, a message, then yanking it solves nothing. It's like my mom. For thirty years she gags herself, puts up with my dad in silence. For three decades she chokes down her anger, and then she's freaked to be diagnosed with *throat* cancer? I mean, how can she possibly be so naive? Even now, even knowing she'll probably pack it in before long, she can't open up. She tries, I know, she cries, she rages. Last week she smashed a bunch of her best dishes, her wedding pattern, the Royal Doulton. Still, she doesn't really get it. Rather than turn to my dad and tell him what a patriarchal son of a bitch he is, she rants at me as though I were the heartless one.

I forgive and release all the hurt I've received. I give myself permission to feel what I feel at each moment. This is the affirmation my mom's supposed to repeat to herself to shrink the tumour. And here's mine: *I am loved and accepted by life. There's a place for me in this world.* This should straighten up my wisdom teeth, and maybe close up the little gap I have here at the front, where Mitch keeps catching his tongue. If I just keep repeating it, over and over again, it will have no choice but to be true.

duSt

“If only I had strangled or drowned,” he says, “on my way down to the bitter light.”

“Mmm . . . *Hamlet*?” she says.

“Pardon me?” he says.

“*Hamlet*? Is that from *Hamlet*?”

“What do you mean?” he says. “What are you talking about?”

“That quote, was it from *Hamlet*?”

“It wasn’t a quote,” he says, “that was me, that’s what I was saying.”

“No it isn’t,” she says. “I know that bit. Are you sure it isn’t . . . Maybe Strindberg. Could be Strindberg. Is it Strindberg?”

“Stop *doing* this,” he says. “Jesus. It was me, I was saying that. I wish to God I’d never been born. I wish—”

“Give me one clue. Come on, one little clue. Was it . . . are we talking about this century?”

"You know, you're really upsetting me now," he says. "I mean it. I'm in a very vulnerable phase, I'm going through a really rough time. I've just lost—"

"Let me hear it again," she says. "Just say it one more time, and I swear I'll get it."

"I don't even remember what I said," he says. "Look, I don't care what I said, it's not what I want to talk about. I want to talk about my—"

"Man or woman? Was it written by a man or a woman? You can tell me that much, it's hardly giving it away."

"I'm going to kill myself, you know that?" he says. "I'm goddam suicidal. Why do you think I called this number? *You're not alone*, the poster says. *We're here to listen.* Well I don't hear much listening going on just at the moment. My heart's broken here, and what I—"

"Was it originally in English? That's all I want to know, English or translation. How about a little patience."

"Just so you know," he says, "I've got everything I need on the bed beside me. I've got Gravol, I've got Seconal, I've got Valium. Plenty. I've got a plastic bag. I've researched this, I know what I'm doing. Don't think I'm some cry-for-help type that won't go through with it, because I will. It'll be over before you find me."

"One more line," she says. "Give me one more line, and if I don't get it I'll say uncle. Cross my heart."

"Ah, silence and peace have abandoned me," he says, "and anguish camps in my heart."

"Job!" she says. "Book of Job! I can't believe it. How could I—"

"Book of what?" he says.

"Book of Job."

"It sounds kind of . . . sad."

"It is," she says, "but it's beautiful, it's so beautiful." She pauses. "You should read it."

"Yeah, maybe," he says. "I will be quiet, comforted that I am dust."

proOf

T

It began innocently enough, it began with me trying to prove the existence of God.

"Animals always evolve for a reason," I said, rolling a stick of chalk between my palms like a playdough snake. "Animals change to fit their world, and that means they represent their world, symbolize their world in a certain way."

This was my good class, my honours grad class, bright, ambitious kids on the brink of adulthood—me a decade ago. I'm always trying to stretch this group, shake them up, tease their minds free of their glands for an hour or two.

"For instance," I said, "imagine you've never been to the plains of Africa, and I suddenly show you a giraffe. What do you notice about it?"

"It's got a long neck," said Brad Jenkins. Odd in itself, he never opens his mouth.

"Right, good, Brad. What else?"

Silence.

"Think of how it eats."

"I'd check its teeth," said Rose Choy, "and see they're flat for, like, grinding. A vegetarian."

"Right, exactly," I said. "So what can you tell me about its world?"

"Tall trees," said Annie Fry, the gawky redhead by the window, one of my best. "Where it lives there must be tall trees."

"Excellent, Annie," I said. "Excellent." I turned to the board. *Long neck, flat teeth—tall trees.* If you don't scrawl something every once in a while the kids tune out. "You know the structure of its body corresponds to its environment," I said, "so you can read its environment off the template of its body. But mustn't the same thing be true of its mind? If an animal develops a certain way of thinking, can't we be just as sure it's mirroring the real world? What would be the point of thinking about something that doesn't exist? We wouldn't have evolved canine teeth, would we, if there were no such thing as meat to sink them into?"

A general, provisional nodding of heads. What the hell's he talking about?

"Take religious faith," I said. "If most of us *Homo sapiens* conceive of something called God, hunger for something called God, doesn't that mean there's such a thing as God out there someplace?"

They looked at me as though I were speaking in tongues.

"Let's go further," I said. "In nature, remember, two interdependent organisms often evolve in tandem. What's that called, Alex? Eva? Martin?"

"Coevolution," said Martin Bain. A jock, and brains to boot—you can't help hating the kid just a little.

"Correct. Nice to know somebody's been listening. So let's assume human beings and God perceive one another, and that they're actually evolving together, responding to one another as they interact. That God is *becoming God* in the same way we're *becoming human*, and at the same time. In synch. The way the beak of a hummingbird, say, and the bell of a blossom evolve in response to one another." I fashioned a beak of my right hand, a blossom of my left. I jammed one into the other. "The blossom grows deeper, so the hummingbird has to thrust deeper to get at its nectar, and thus pick up more pollen. Right? So the beak of the hummingbird grows longer, and the blossom grows deeper, and the beak of the hummingbird grows longer, and the blossom grows deeper, and the beak of the hummingbird grows longer, and the blossom grows deeper. . . . Who can think of another example? Annie?"

That's when it happened. Well, nothing actually happened until much later of course, but that was the moment, the instant in which the hunger stirred. Annie was eighteen, there was nothing remotely illegal. Still.

I miss the teaching, sure, but that isn't it. There's something else.

pRovisions

So Jessica comes home from school today, she's in grade three, and asks what we plan to take with us when we go away. What *provisions*, is how she puts it, with that you'd-better-be-taking-me-seriously expression she gets on. It's an only-child thing, I think.

Carol one-eyebrows me across the dinner table. "Go where again, Jess?"

"Away," she says.

"Away, hon?" I say.

"You know. When the bombs."

It was Danny McGowan, I gather, who raised his hand (easing his finger, first, from the slick silo of his nose) to ask Ms. Gilligan what we were supposed to do when somebody pushed a button someplace and the bombs started pelting down. Danny's dad had a whopper of a panic attack last night, apparently, when he found out how many missiles there still are aimed at how many cities—how much more dangerous it is now that the other guys don't *give* a shit. Serves him right for watching the news, poor bastard. Ended up in emerg.

Anyway, Ms. Gilligan—Ms. Three-Hour-Tour, as Carol and I now call her—calmly explained that we'll all have to go away someplace safe for a while. Someplace wild and remote, a sort of mass camping trip, is how she depicted it. The kids went mad. War broke out over who got to share a tent with whom, whose dad would stagger back to camp under a bigger load of venison, and whether Malcolm Grailey—a shrill, brown-nosed little pain in the butt by all accounts—should be invited along at all. Ms. Gilligan, hoping to simmer things down, broke the news that life wouldn't be quite the same when we came back to civilization. "Yipee!" was the unanimous response. "Yahoo!" Not *at all* the same, Ms. Gilligan persisted. In fact, everything would probably be gone. "Poof," she even said, according to Jessica.

It was Jessica, then, that little miracle of practicality (some very, very recessive gene well hidden in her mother and me) who said, "We'll have to take stuff with us. Food and clothes and all that stuff."

"Not stuff," said Ms. Gilligan, and she wheeled to face the board. "P-r-o-v-i-s-i-o-n-s," she intoned over the scraping of her chalk. "Provisions. Things . . . you . . . take . . . with . . . you . . . when . . . you . . . go. Copy it into your notebooks, class. And Danny, just kindly get that finger . . ."

So we spend the evening compiling our list. *Absoloot Nesessaries*, is how Jessica starts it off (she got her mother's spelling, sadly). No video games, no fuzzy bed-buddies, not for this kid. *Canned goods*, she keeps stressing, we'll need lots of *canned goods*. When I think of Armageddon from now on I'll think of brown beans, of cold Alphaghetti. For breakfast it'll be some sort of whole grain glop, for lunch fresh berries and bannock. Carol's gummi bears are history, ditto my marshmallow cookies.

School books, of course, have made the nesessaries list. Jessica has no intention of *falling behind*, as she puts it. Her piano's out of the question, so she'll have to make do with her recorder, and patch together some sort of wilderness choir. There's bound to be a flat rock for her tap dancing, and she'll keep up her diaries—sorry, journals—on sheets of birchbark with chunks of charred wood from the fire.

"What will the weather be like?" she wonders.

Calling to mind the nuclear winter concept I tell her, "Chilly."

So, extra sweaters. Long johns. Toques. Mittens. I imagine Jess bundling Carol and me into snow suits, mummying us in tasseled scarves. Snowflakes alight on our eyelids, our cheeks, each one unique for the instant before it melts.

"Stand still, for goodness' sake," Jess is saying, dabbing at our runny noses, "Stand *still.*"

suiTe

T

"Does it turn you on?" says the woman. "It turns me on in a funny kind of way." She lies on her back in bed, staring at the ceiling. "It sounds as though they're going to come right through."

"Honey, I'm reading," says the man. He grasps a book in both hands, a formidable book, balancing it on his bare, almost hairless chest and angling it so that it collects light from the bedside lamp. He's read the same phrase seven times now—*To procreate is to vanish*—and still can't get it.

The thumping and moaning from the second-floor suite subsides briefly—shift in position, presumably—and then starts up again, accompanied by the sound of a crowd roaring, a reggae beat rising.

"'No Woman' . . ." says the woman.

". . . 'No Cry,'" says the man. He slaps his book shut with a sigh, sets it on the bedside table. "Only song that really takes him there, I guess. Same one? Dark, skinny?"

"She's not that skinny," says the woman. "But I mean, do you find sex . . . sexy? Does it make you want to join in?"

The man swivels his head in her direction.

"Passenger pigeons?" she says. "At the end, when there were only a few of them left? They wouldn't mate. They needed to be all doing it together, a bunch of them, a collective thing. Fecundity."

"Fecundity?"

"Fecundity. Oop, I think she's getting close."

They lie still together, listening.

"False alarm," he says.

"Put something on," she says. She kisses him on the shoulder. "The Verdi. I'll be right back."

The man watches as she sweeps out of bed and strides across to the bathroom, shucking her nightshirt on the way. Without rising he reaches over to the stereo, pushes a button. By the time she returns he's adjusted the volume so that it just blots out the Wailers.

"*Misterioso*," says the woman in the basement suite, slipping the tasseled bookmark back into her murder mystery. "Are you awake, honey?"

"*Misterioso altero, croce, croce e delizia*," says the man sleepily beside her. "Sadness with pleasure blended."

She's already got the Betty Carter tape loaded when the banging from up above really kicks in, enriching the complex of rhythms.

"All the Things You Are," he murmurs. He rolls onto her, reaching for the light, and they vanish.

oranGe

T

I've made a deal with myself. I'll call her once and once only, after each pint, from the pay phone in the lobby. If there's still no answer when I'm too drunk to dial, forget it. I'm drinking faster than normal—after about an hour I've already ordered my fourth pint. My limit is three.

The guy at the next table over is waxing philosophical, damn near shouting over the din of conversation and canned hits from the eighties. "I don't give a crap," he says. He and his buddy have just struck out with the two silky blouses at the bar. "I've already slept with everybody anyway."

"Yeah, exactly," says his buddy. And then, after a pause, "What do you mean?"

"I've already slept with everybody," says the philosopher. His big blond hair is flattened on one side, as though he has in fact just jimmied himself out of bed. "I've slept with everybody in this crummy place, that's for damn sure. So have you, I'll bet."

"Damn rights," says his buddy. And then, on second thought, "No I haven't."

Sue returns with my pint. "Thanks," I say.

"My pleasure, hon," she says. "Where's your friend tonight?"

I shrug, lay down my money. She moves on, glutes flexing under red leather.

"Think about it," the philosopher is saying. "Every time you sleep with somebody you're sleeping with everybody they've ever slept with, too. You've heard that, haven't you? When some woman's trying to talk you into wearing your little raincoat?"

"Yeah, I guess."

"Sure you have," says the philosopher. "So, how many women have you slept with?"

"I don't know."

"Take a guess," says the philosopher. "Give me an estimate."

"I told you, I don't fucking *know*," says his buddy. He removes his ball cap, works the bill into a more fetching arch, and lowers it once more over his eyes.

"Okay, okay," says the philosopher. "Take it easy. Let's say you've slept with ten women."

"Bullshit, I've slept with a hell of a lot more women than that."

"Fine, we're being conservative here. Now, say each of those ten women has already slept with ten men. On average. Fair enough?"

"Whatever."

"That means you've slept with a hundred and ten people," says the philosopher, "and a hundred of them are guys."

"Fuck you," says his buddy.

"But each of those hundred guys has already slept with ten other women," says the philosopher. "That's a thousand. And each of those thousand women has already slept with ten other guys. That's ten thousand. And each of those ten thousand guys has already slept with ten women. That's a hundred thousand."

"What the fuck are you talking about?"

"But wait," says the philosopher. "Each of those hundred thousand guys has slept with ten other women, that's a million. And each of those million women has slept with ten other guys, that's ten million. Get the idea?"

"No."

I'm only halfway through my pint, but what the hey. I head for the lobby, planting my feet with a little more care than usual. There's a woman on the telephone already, an incredibly tall woman in an incredibly short orange skirt and orange high heels.

She says into the telephone, "Why don't you all come down?"

A guy bursts out of the can, a great hulking blur of denim and muscle. He catches me gaping, appears to contemplate, briefly, beating the crap out of me, and then lurches back into the bar.

"What?" says the tall woman. "I can't hear you." Pause. "No, you come *here*. You come *here*. Yeah. Okay. Bye." She totters into the women's room.

My turn. I've got the number by heart now. Three rings, four.

"Hello?" she says.

"Oh, hi," I say. "It's me."

"Me?"

"Me."

"Oh, hi," she says.

I have no idea what to say. I must have had a plan, but what was it? I say, "Does anything rhyme with orange?"

"*What?*" she says.

"Hang on," I say, "that's not it. Do you believe you're meant to love one person? I mean, one particular person, one special person? Or do you believe you could love just anybody?"

"Are you drunk?" she says. "You're drunk."

"Hang on," I say, "that's not it."

magiC

T

The most infuriating thing is that he still gets them in the middle of the night, sometimes, while he and Mona are zonked out and they're absolutely no use to anybody. Jim's a fitful sleeper—he'll flip onto his front and moments later stir from a dream in which he's being jabbed in the belly with a magic wand. "Three wishes?" he'll be saying. "Why only three wishes? Oh, wait, wait, my first wish is to have an infinite number of wishes—"

Fully awake, then, he'll take the thing tentatively in hand. Vibrant as a spring sapling, hot as a sun-baked steering wheel. "I wish—" But by then it'll be gone. Poof. Magic.

Mona's been very understanding. In other words she's been tolerant, even though she understands nothing. What's to understand? It's there or it isn't, it arises or it doesn't. The whole business is a perfect mystery, as uncanny and inconceivable as the waxing and waning of the moon, as the ebb and flow of her own blood currents, which grow more irregular now with each passing month. It's age, time. Loony is what it'll drive you if you let it.

Jim is taking a little longer to come around to this view, to achieve this level of acquiescence. For several months now he's put his faith in hard work. Greater effort, more refined concentration. He had a go at push-ups for a start, sit-ups, knee-bends. He'd do a set of each first thing in the morning, a set of each last thing at night, climbing straight into bed all huffy and hot. Nothing.

Then aerobics, an "Eiffel Tower" stairclimber, a "Coxswain" rowing machine. Zip.

Never one for metaphysics, Jim nonetheless graduated to a more occult approach, specifically to a New Age brand of fantasy called "creative visualization." He'd read about it in one of Mona's well-thumbed glossies, under the title "What About When *He's* Got a Headache?" Jim adopted the practice of kneeling by the bed each night—while Mona pursued her own fragrant wizardry behind the bathroom door—seeking to silence, briefly, the fizzing mob scene of his mind. A shot or two of whisky beforehand seemed to help. He'd conjure an image of Mona, a certain sweaty clip in which she performed one of the tricks he'd always dreamed of teaching her, a balancing act with Jim as beam. When even this failed to get a rise out of him he began including swift, salacious cameos by his aerobics instructor, a bleached-blonde, one-breasted Amazon, who's been cartwheeling nightly through their silent bedroom ever since. Long after he and Mona have crawled under the blankets these images keep Jim wide awake, but leave the somnolent member undisturbed.

The magic wand is back tonight, in Jim's very first dream. This time, though, he's managed to get a grip on it. The woman wielding it—Mona, but not—tries to wrestle it back from him. She wears a crinoline good-witch getup which crackles with each to and fro.

"Let go," she says, pulling the wand her way.

"No," he says, pulling it his way.

"Yes."

"No."

"Yes."

"No."

"Yes, yes . . . *yes.*"

Jim wakes up just as Mona collapses, crying out, onto his chest. Her hair covers his face, filigreeing the moonlight. Her breath comes in hot gusts against his neck, a wordless incantation, a binding spell.

"I wish . . ."

"Wish what, honey?" she murmurs.

But he still can't say.

T

the pOint of dreaming

Here's the suicide note I'd like to have written:

> *Honey, it wasn't you. Please, please believe this, whatever else you choose to believe. I've been as happy with you as I could have been with anyone, and that was almost happy enough.*
>
> *As for your dream last night, it was no presentiment, no premonition. Believe this too. Seeing yourself dead is a good omen, actually, it promises a long and prosperous life. That's what the ancient Egyptians believed, anyway, and they were all over this kind of thing. Incidentally, a dream about sex with a cow is another good omen, in case you're ever desperate for one (a good omen, I mean, not a cow).*

All these years I've tried to make her laugh, why would I quit now?

> *I always loved listening to your dreams in the morning, sweetheart, while I was suiting up for the world and you were still enshrouded in your sheaf of blankets ("Weight," you'd cry out in the night, "give me more weight!"). God knows I could never remember my own dreams. What does this say about a man, that he can't remember his dreams? Very little, I suspect. But if this is true, if it doesn't much matter whether or not we recall them, why do we bother having them in the first place? What's the point of dreaming?*
>
> *The point of dreaming is to keep us asleep. That's what Sigmund Freud believed, anyway, and he was all over this kind of thing. Dreams are meant to drain off the extra energy that would otherwise disturb us from our slumber. Dreams are like movies, they're like books, they're meant to give us the impression something's happening when it really isn't. Only occasionally do dreams fail us, allow a spike of adrenaline to penetrate the bubble of our passivity. In a dream of falling, say ...*
>
> *Honey, I want to wake up. Here's what I imagine, I imagine that as the ground comes hurtling up at me, as gravity gathers me swiftly into its arms I'll suddenly jerk myself free, I'll finally snap out of it. And I'll awake to some greater, clearer, cleaner life.*

As I say, that's the note I'd like to have written, and left for my wife on the kitchen table underneath the "I'd Rather Be Sailing!" mug. With perhaps a little epigraph from John Donne—"One short sleep past, we wake eternally"—to jack up the intellectual quotient.

There are two reasons I failed to write this note. The first is that I had no intention of killing myself. I was up on the roof of our townhouse (three stories, wouldn't you know it) to fix the damn skylight, not to jump. Sure, I'd toyed with the idea of suicide from time to time, but who hasn't? Flirted is the word, I'd flirted with the idea of suicide in much the same way I'd flirted with the idea of seducing our neighbour's nineteen-year-old daughter—the same nineteen-year-old daughter whose sleek, oil-slathered physique I could see from the roof, by the way, doing the rotisserie thing out on their patio, and who in a sense can be held responsible for my lack of concentration, and thus for my fall. I'd never actually have killed myself, any more than I'd actually have seduced the girl. Sex and death, these were idle fantasies, they were dreams—again, the whole point of them was to keep me from doing anything rash. I had a wife, I had a job, I had a house—townhouse, then—I had a brother, I had a father, and so on. I had a thousand things to keep me alive, or at least to make me ashamed of the idea of giving up.

So that's one reason. The second reason is that I didn't *know*, I had no *idea*. And now I can't tell her.

T the perfection of the moMent

Note to self: Next time you're walking alone late at night on a deserted downtown street lined with darkened shops and some drunken goon leans out of a pickup truck shouting, "Hey, faggot!" do *not* blow him a kiss. Consider these alternate courses of action: Pray. Play deaf. Pull out your keys and approach the nearest doorway, as though to let yourself in. Pull out your wallet, flip it open and begin barking urgently into it as though it were a cell phone, the cell phone your girlfriend's been pestering you to pick up for these past six months. Run like a sonofabitch.

Note to self: Next time you blow a kiss at some drunken goon in a pickup truck, pissing him off so much that he pulls over to beat the bejesus out of you, do *not* go into that ludicrous kung fu stance you got off the television. Rather, run like a sonofabitch.

Note to self: Next time some drunken goon is beating the bejesus out of you and you manage to tip him over, briefly, do *not* presume that this trivial, fleeting victory is a consequence of your power and prowess, and most definitely do *not* snap at him, "Who's the faggot now, you sad-assed, milque-toasted motherfucker?" Bear in mind that this is a drunken goon you're dealing with, a goon so drunken that he collapsed twice on his way from pickup truck to you. Bear in mind, too, that there may be another drunken goon in the pickup truck, a bigger and slightly less drunken drunken goon.

Note to self: Next time a bigger and slightly less drunken drunken goon clambers out of a pickup truck and charges you with an empty forty-ouncer raised, club-like, over his head, do *not* launch into a wordy explanation of your status vis-à-vis sexuality. Consider the possibility that he won't be impressed by tales of your success, such as it is, with women. Consider—better late than never—running like a sonofabitch.

Note to self: Next time some drunken goon has clonked you with an empty forty-ouncer and you're getting your head stitched up at the hospital, do *not* remark to the doctor, "It would be one thing if I actually *were* a faggot." Consider the possibility that the doctor, who's currently passing a needle through your flesh, will have a personal reason for taking offense at this comment. Consider the statistic you came upon recently in an article on the nature/nurture debate with regard to homosexuality. Consider how your luck has gone so far this evening.

Note to self: Next time a doctor, passing a needle through your flesh, takes offense at some moronic aside you've just let slip, do *not* try to salvage the situation by announcing, "A lot of my best friends are gay," even if there's a smidgeon of truth to this statement. Rather, feign the symptoms of concussion. Realize you don't actually need to feign such symptoms, since in fact you're feeling woozy, disoriented.

Note to self: Next time your girlfriend is driving you home from the hospital where you've had your head stitched up and she says to you, "You know, I actually thought you were gay the first time we met," do *not* snap back at her, "Yeah, well, you've always struck me as pretty goddam butch." Instead, attempt to construe her remark as a compliment, a fond reference to your sublime sensitivity, the chumminess you've achieved with your anima, your inner female, that sort of thing. Consider saying, "Thank you."

Note to self: Next time your girlfriend has forgiven you for referring to her as "butch," and she's tucked you into bed with an icepack on your head and a hot water bottle under your back, and she's kissing her way down your chest, down your belly, and you get the sense you're in for some serious lovin', do *not* begin to wonder if there isn't actually something ever so slightly masculine about her—the squared-off jaw, the broad brow—whether this isn't part of the attraction, and whether those drunken goons mightn't actually have been onto something. Rather, abandon yourself to the annihilating perfection of the moment.

liCorice

T

"I have a theory," says my friend Craig. Craig always has a theory, or no, he always has two theories, a pair of theories pulling him in precisely opposite directions, with precisely equal force. Like two guy wires, let's say, or better yet two lassoes, two lariats around a bull's neck holding it immobile. Immobility is the state for which Craig is always striving.

"I have a theory," says Craig. We're sitting in a crowded movie theatre, Craig and I. There's an empty seat between us. Craig's wife, Kim, has just dashed out for treats. When I have a date we often make a foursome, but it's been a while, so tonight they're letting me tag along alone. Kim chose the flick, a weepy about a modern working woman torn by conflicting passions. It'll start any minute.

"I have a theory," says Craig, one more time.

"Craig, just spit it *out*," I say. "What's your theory?"

"Funny you should ask," he says. "But you can't tell Kim."

"How dare you," I say. "How dare you deprive a single—"

"I'm serious."

"All right, all right. Cross my heart."

"Here's my theory, then." He quick-looks left and right. "My theory is that a man's search for the truth about his wife—what she's really doing when he isn't around—is the model, the prototype for all truth-seeking. Science, philosophy, you name it. That's where it all started, a man worrying about who else might be having his woman."

"I see," I say. I crane my neck—no Kim. "How so?"

"Infidelity is the truth," he says. "Everyone and everything, in the end, is unfaithful."

"Hmm."

"Infidelity," he says, "is life's metaphor for mortality."

"Interesting." Is this what I'd normally say?

"You really think so?" Would he normally ask?

"Sure," I say. "Only, there's something, I don't know . . ."

"Missing?" he says.

"Yeah, missing," I say.

"I think so too," he says. He looks relieved. "Because there's something just as valuable as the search for truth. Maybe even more valuable."

"What's that?" I say. "Here comes Kim."

"The surrender to mystery," he says. "Knowing you can't know."

"Right," I say. "I guess that's it."

"Just in time," says Kim as she squeezes past me to her seat. The backs of her bare legs brush my knees. Music comes up, tense and percussive, a runner for an upcoming thriller.

And Kim, "Licorice?"

the end of the dAy

"'*See what you have done!' she screamed,*" I recite in my Daddy-voice. " '*In a minute I shall melt away.' 'I'm very sorry, indeed,' said Dorothy, who was truly frightened to see the Witch actually melting away like brown sugar before her very—*"

"She isn't really," says Suze.

"Hmm?" I say. "Isn't really what, honey?" My mind has moseyed off again.

"Sorry," says Suze. "About a horrid old witch? Good riddance." She hoists a hillock of bubbles up on her pudgy palm, blows it away. "Now she'll free the Winkies and get back to the Emerald City."

"Hm," I say. "How do you come to know so much about these things?"

"You've only read this to me ten zillion times, Dad. Keep going."

"How about a little hair washing first."

"Finish first. We're almost—"

"Hair washing, then story reading," I say. "That's how it goes, that's how the Good Witch of the South would have wanted it."

"North," says Suze.

"Whatever." The phone emits its horrible little cry—a bloodless bleating—out in the hall. I give it a moment, hoping somebody else will pick up, my wife or my boy. "Right back, sweetie," I say.

"No, stay. I'll—"

"Soap that hair. I'll be right back."

It's Arthur, fretting about our meeting tomorrow. "I'm not ready for this," he says. "Jesus, what have I gotten myself into?"

"Arthur, relax," I say. "You say your bit, I back you up. It's a slam dunk."

"I don't know," he says. "I've been . . . You don't think Lange's been a little, maybe, short with me? Ever since that thing with Cunningham I feel like—"

"Arthur, you're being an idiot," I say. "I gotta go. I'll see you in the eh em."

"Yeah, you're right," he says. "All right. See you then."

I hang up, stand staring down at the phone a moment. I'm weary, waiting for the end of the day. "You scrubbed in there?" I say, shuffling back into the bathroom's fragrant fog.

"Dad!" says Suze. She looks startled—as do I, I suppose. She has a pink plastic razor in one hand, and the other's behind her head, elbow raised to reveal a sudsy underarm. The bubblebath has been unbubbling—Suze slides down so that the dark cradle of her cleavage largely disappears from view.

"Emerald City," I say.

"Pardon?" says Suze.

I peer down at my empty hands. "Winkies?" I say.

"Um, Dad," says Suze.

Something needs to be set right, this much is clear. "Suze, I'm sorry," I say.

It doesn't seem enough, somehow. So many things I could have done better. "I'm awfully, *awfully* sorry."

"It's okay, Dad," she says.
But I'm not so sure.

kaNsas

The night Cam first met Cynthia, six years ago now, he wasn't himself. He was Kurt Gödel, the mathematician responsible for destroying mathematics, or at least for destroying the mathematician's dream of completeness, of wholeness. And he was halfway drunk.

"Dorothy?" he said. He'd been at the party a couple of hours already—a post-midterm affair, an obligatory blow-out—shouldering through crowded rooms as though he had somebody special to search for.

"Actually, I'm Judy," said Cynthia, swinging her wicker picnic basket, scruffling the head of her toy Toto.

"You mean, Judy Garland?" said Cam.

"Yeah, as Dorothy," said Cynthia, nodding. "Just before she shoots the sleepy scene in the field of poppies." She pursed her lips, appraising Cam's costume in the pale smoky light. "Judy was sixteen trying to look thirteen," she said. "They had to flatten her boobs. I'm twenty-two trying to look sixteen trying to look thirteen."

Cam snuck a peek down at Cynthia's breasts, modest mounds straining against her girlish smock. Does she know I'm in the math department, is that it? "Divide by two add five," he said, feeling foolish. "I'm twenty-two too, by the way." And then, "Hey, wasn't she Gumm? Wasn't she born Frances Gumm?"

"Right," said Cynthia. She smiled, sipped her beer from its bottle. The Marquis de Sade stumbled past, flicked her with his riding crop. "Fuck off, Fujio," she said, still smiling. Funny little pointed teeth.

"I'm Cam," said Cam. He went to drink from his own bottle, found it empty.

"Cynthia." She reached out and snapped one of his straps. "My mother wore one of those, but *under* her clothes."

Cam shrugged. "It's a pun, a really bad pun. I'm supposed to be Kurt Gödel, the mathematician. That's how you say it, the O with the umlaut. Girdle?"

Cynthia nodded. "That's a good pun, actually. What was his thing, Gödel's thing? But bearing in mind I'm in the English department."

Cam took another pull at his empty bottle. Somebody had just cranked up the tunes, early Genesis, "Carpet Crawlers." Cam was suddenly feeling very good. *You gotta get in to get out . . .* "Gödel proved that all systems contain undecidable propositions," he shouted, leaning in, "that no system can be both consistent and complete." Joan of Arc waved her sword at him from across the room—a guy from one of his tutorials in a little green tunic. Cam waved back. "Gödel said you'll never be able to capture it all," he shouted, "that even when you've said everything, you haven't said everything. You've left something out."

Cynthia scowled. "Another effing poet," she yelled, her breath a weird brew of garlic and hops. "I'm up to here with poets. Got any more beer?"

"'Fraid not. Drank it all."

"Wait here," she yelled. "I'll get us some."

Cam did something with his face that said, "How?"

Cynthia smiled up at him—she was shortish, almost munchkinish next to Cam's lanky six three—and gave her body the subtlest little shimmy.

"I'll wait here," he shouted.

In the morning he found himself spooned up against her on their host's living room couch. The room looked as though it had been hit by a twister, and was in fact still spinning—Cynthia had scored big-time on her booze-trolling tour, and they'd kept at it, yacking, drinking, dancing, almost until dawn. Cam was still in his girdle, though a strap or two had snapped. His hand had tunneled its way up under Cynthia's blouse to her tummy. She stirred.

Cynthia said, "I have the feeling . . ."

". . . we're not in Kansas any more," said Cam.

It was one of those moments, one of those rare moments that hint at a sort of completeness, of wholeness. One of those moments pregnant with totality.

And this is another. Cam has his hand on her tummy again, which is swollen, tight.

"Don't push," he's saying. "It isn't time to push yet."

Her face is drenched with sweat, her mouth gaping like an angry god's. She's herself and much more than herself, both. "*Ungggbaerrr!*" she says. English major.

"Wait, honey, wait," says Cam. Hold it.

Do the math

T

"Eight hundred thousand people," says Brad, the young man offering up this evening's slide show. He reminds me of my son, Bret—about the same age, some of that same manic romanticism about him. And then the name thing. "Try to imagine the amount of brutality required to murder, by machete, eight hundred thousand people."

Please. I'm not big on stereotypes but let's face it, I'm a middle-aged, middle-class white man. I've never suffered anything more violent than a scuffle in a ticket queue. I'm comfortably ensconced just now—complete with snifter—in an Edwardian wing chair by a fireplace in a recently renovated character home in a quiet residential neighbourhood of a white-as-a-ghost western city. How likely is it I'll be able to imagine the amount of brutality required to murder, by machete, eight hundred thousand people?

Then again, I do like a challenge. Remember, I'm a middle-aged, middle-class white man.

The slide Brad currently has up on the screen depicts one of the eight hundred thousand, clearly. He's a man, or he was—his body rots now by the side of a road. For some unthinkable reason he wears his shoes on his hands. His limbs fly off in all directions, articulated in all the wrong places—we might be gazing at some ancient hieroglyphic, a cryptic black squiggle on the rumpled parchment of mother earth. But we're not.

It occurs to me—a momentary flash of brilliance—that if I could only imagine the amount of brutality required to murder, by machete, this one man, then I'd already be halfway to meeting my challenge. I'd just do the math, I'd take this amount of brutality and I'd multiply it by eight hundred thousand. But how to perform this first calculation? How to assess the amount of brutality required to murder, by machete, this one man? I suppose I'll have to work from my own experience somehow. Extrapolate.

It's not easy concentrating on any of this, mind you, with the slide show still clunking along. We've moved on to a shot of a stack of skulls now—brings to mind the relics of saints down in the catacombs, from that class trip we took to Rome when I was a kid. Next, some sort of mass burial site, where women kneel and weep. One of the women is pregnant—a Tutsi woman carrying a Hutu child, we are told. She appears to be making the sign of the cross. Can this be true?

"Rape is one of the most potent tools of genocide," Brad explains. "Rape can be even more brutal than the machete." This fact seems more likely to complicate than to clarify my calculations. I set it aside for the moment.

I know very little about brutality, as I've already confessed. Anger, though, I could fill you in about anger. I'm pretty goddam angry right this minute, as a matter of fact. Since my divorce was finally nailed down—ten weeks ago this coming Tuesday—people have been coercing me into every blessed social event they can cobble together. Making her pitch for this evening's affair, my friend Ginny had lots to say about the "authentic" African meal she'd be serving—coconut bean soup and duckling *dar es salaam*—and about Brad's "wonderful slide presentation," his "stunning photography." The small matter of genocide seems to have slipped her mind.

I hate this, I really do. I hate having all this horrendous imagery thrust at me, all this pain against which I'm completely powerless. Should I tell her? What if, instead of simply glowering at her as I've been doing for the last few minutes, I were to snarl, "Dammit, Ginny, you had no right!"? What if I were to slam down my snifter so that it splashed brandy all over her brand new, buff-coloured carpet? How much brutality would that require? Given the right circumstances, the right incentives, is it possible that a person could employ this same amount of brutality to murder—by machete, say—one man? I wonder. And I wonder if, one man having been murdered by machete, the murder of the next man by machete mightn't require even less brutality, and the man after that even less, and so on. It seems likely, all of a sudden, that my whole approach to this question has been simpleminded, that a far more complex calculation is called for. Some higher math, some arcane equation I may have been capable of grasping, momentarily, about twenty years ago.

"The worst of it is, we knew," Brad is saying. "Months of planning go into something like this—we knew about it all along. We knew, and we did nothing. Try to imagine the depth of denial, the depth of cynicism involved in turning away from this kind of suffering."

So here we go again.

priSoner

Imprisoned for a crime you can scarcely comprehend—though you've committed others, of course, and far worse—you determine to educate, to expand yourself. To release yourself with language. You'll learn a new word every day, inflate your vocabulary like a great orbicular balloon (goodness, what a wonderful start you've made!), a great domical dirigible that will pluck you from your feet, hoist you over these barbed-wire walls. Who knows where it will allow itself to be steered? Not you. How could you know when you're not able to say?

Time to bear down, get to work.

You pilfer the dictionary from the prison library. You begin methodically. *A. Aah. Aardvark. Aardwolf.* All the way to *abaca*, "a fibre obtained from the leafstalk of a banana native to the Philippines—called also Manila hemp." In search of *hemp* you come upon *henotheism*, "the worship of one god without denying the existence of other gods." You determine to use this word in a sentence, to burn it more deeply into your cortical . . . whatever (do words fail you, or do you fail them?). During exercise hour one day you amble up to a fellow inmate, natural as can be. "Do you think we should all be praising Allah?" you say. "Or are you a henotheist?"

In the infirmary you have time to pore (with your one remaining good eye) over the dictionary at considerable length. You reach *transgression* by way of *guilt*, which you reach by way of *prisoner*. Odd that you should reach anything at all by way of *prisoner*; since a *prisoner* is pretty much a dead end. This would seem to constitute *irony* 3a(1), "incongruity between the actual result of a sequence of events and the normal or expected result."

You notice that the dictionary, at about two inches deep, has no trouble at all passing between the bars of the infirmary door, so it can come and go at its leisure. You can't, however. You're too thick.

Hegira, you discover, is another word for an exodus or escape. *Transhumance* means "the seasonal movement of livestock, esp. sheep, between mountain and lowland pastures." A *nucellus* is "the central and chief part of a plant ovule that contains the embryo sac." To *keen* is "to lament or mourn loudly."

There seem to be an infinite number of words—but can this really be the case?

You flip to *infinite*, "extending indefinitely, subject to no limitation." You plan to use this word, too, in a sentence, but you can't think of one. The doctor comes by, and you say to him, "What's a sentence containing the word *infinite*?"

"There are lots of them," he says. "But they're all questions. Like yours. How many fingers?"

And he holds them up for you, four little bars rooted in flesh.

all mystEries

T

"Red," said my father.

"Favourite colour . . . red," said Mr. Arnot, licking his pencil and making note of this morsel of information on his little yellow pad. "Now when you say *red*, Mr. James, you're thinking rose red, are you? Ruby red? Blood red?"

"Wine red," said my father. Ornery old bastard, it was his liver that was giving out.

"Wine red," repeated Mr. Arnot. "And your favourite place? I'm wondering about a natural location, now, a favourite lake or mountain or—"

"French River," said my father. "Sheer rock, fast water. Took my boy there to learn to paddle, portage, lug a pack. Make a man of him, ha." It was my father's practice to speak of me as though I were down the hall. Even when we were trapped alone together—as we'd been in that godforsaken canoe, for instance—

I felt as though I were eavesdropping. "If I'd of had grandchildren," he added, "I'd of taken them there too."

"I see, very good," said Mr. Arnot. Mr. Arnot was not only the proprietor and sole salesman, but also the potter, the craftsman behind "You've Urned It." A squinty accountant with artisan's hands. His ad in the *Sunshower News* had boasted of "Customized Creations," so Mr. Arnot was here at the Sunshower Care Facility today to get to know my father, to "soak up a little of his essence," as Mr. Arnot himself had put it over the telephone. This urn was guaranteed to fit my father like a tailored suit. It would also cost a few bucks less than any of the other vessels I'd picked out in recent years, to hold relics of various friends. This assured it of my father's blessing.

"Now, just to help me get a better sense of you, Mr. James," Mr. Arnot went on, "let me ask you this. If you were an animal, what kind of animal would you be?"

"What kind of *animal?*" said my father. He was sitting on the end of his bed in his dressing gown, a scruffy, shrunken creature—an otter in an oil slick, say. He puffed up a little as he said this, though. Indignation had always suited him.

"Well, yes," said Mr. Arnot apologetically. "You see, if I know what kind of animal—"

"I *am* an animal, you dolt," snapped my father, "that's why I'm in this goddam mess."

"Quite so, quite so," said Mr. Arnot. He made a little note on his pad—I'd have died to see it. "Now, just one more thing," he said. "Words. Are there any words you'd . . . Is there any special saying, any quote . . ."

"No," said my father. "Wait. One Corinthians."

"Pardon me?" said Mr. Arnot.

"One Corinthians," said my father.

"Like, in the *Bible?*" I said. My father had never, to my knowledge, quoted from scripture in all his life. Unless you counted "Let there be light," which he used to murmur to himself sometimes as he struck a match for his pipe, or "Consider the lilies," which he'd cry out in ludicrous rapture as he strolled around the back yard half lit, smoking and admiring the pathetic garden my mother tried to keep up. He was not, as far as I'd ever been able to detect, a remotely religious man. His objection to my "lifestyle" was based on other considerations.

"Damn right," he said.

"I don't quite ..." said Mr. Arnot. "Could you just refresh ..."

"*And though I have the gift of prophecy,*" said my father, "*and understand all mysteries, and all knowledge, and though I have all faith, so that I could move mountains, and have not love, I am nothing.*"

"Lovely," said Mr. Arnot. "Just lovely. Now, I wonder if we might shorten it just a trifle. We don't want our urn looking cluttered."

"Who the Jesus hell is *we*?" said my father. "What's this *our*? How many people are you planning to cram in there?"

"Father," I said.

"Mr. James," said Mr. Arnot, "I intended no—"

"Fine, shorten it," said my father. "Just keep in the mountains."

Depending on which way you swivel it on our crowded mantel—depending on which way Mrs. Sanchez sets it when she's done dusting all our urns and jars and finely embossed boxes—Niklas and I are faced with one of two slabs of text on my father's pot. *I could move mountains. I am nothing.* They drift there on that wine-red river, beneath those towering cliffs, bits of wreckage awaiting survivors.

what you're ready fOr

"Have you ever asked yourself why this moment is called the present?" says Dr. Laird. "I'd like you to think about that now."

Dr. Laird runs a hand intently through his whitecap of neat, wavy hair—the kind of hair you'd expect of an upwardly mobile prophet, the kind of hair Moses might have worn if he hadn't died in the desert but had made it to the promised land, retired and hit the lecture circuit. Edgar O. Laird, PhD, esteemed author, therapist and guru, takes another step towards his studio audience, towards the dazzled eye of the camera. He spreads his hands, palms out—no tricks. "Why is this moment called the present? Can anybody tell me?"

Up and down the raked rows heads shake, faces adopt a flummoxed, expectant look. The answer to Dr. Laird's question, by the way, is yes. Any one of us could tell him exactly why this moment is called the present—Dr. Laird explained it to us just moments ago, before one of the cameras went kaput and we had to start again. Besides, most of us are so steeped in the wise man's writings that he'd have a devil of a time stumping us. His nifty mnemonics help us out, naturally. I'M MORE: I'm Making My Own Reality Everyday. I CAN: I'm Calling for Abundance Now. GIMME: God Is Making More for Everyone. Still, we wear expressions of unfeigned and delighted anticipation. We're enjoying the shtick even more now that we're in on it.

"Let me tell you then," Dr. Laird finally relents. He tugs back the sleeves of his woolen turtleneck, exposing two thick, furry forearms—getting down to business. "This moment, this now"—he effects a scooping motion with his hands, gathering in the instant like a great pile of poker chips—"this *present* is a *gift*." And he clutches it to his chest.

An appreciative murmur ripples through the audience, a collective sigh of wonder and assent. Heads list ever so slightly right or left in wistful rumination. Present . . . gift . . . This guy's good.

"As a matter of fact," Dr. Laird continues, "now isn't just a gift, it's *the* gift. If you don't take anything else away with you tonight, I'd like you to take this, the knowledge that this moment is your only possession. It's a difficult knowledge, a demanding knowledge, but you're ready for it. How do I know this? I know this because if you weren't ready for what I have to teach you . . . *you wouldn't be here tonight!* It's that simple. If you weren't ready, you wouldn't be here. The car would have broken down, the sitter would have canceled. Do you see what I'm saying? The world gives each one of us just exactly what we're ready for. I have to tell you, I was on a retreat recently in the Catskills with Ben Roshi, the great Jewish Zen master. Incredible man, Ben is, a true Bodhisattva." The doctor's tone has modulated here, from oracular to avuncular—he's ready to share a little anecdote. A cameraman darts forward with a handheld unit to impart an intimate feel to the footage.

"I'd just been meditating for about eighteen hours," Dr. Laird continues, "and I stopped into the hotel's reception area to pick up a fax. Ben was there doing the same thing. We had a good laugh—it's the sages who really see how funny it all is, you know. Anyway—"

"Okay, Dr. Laird," comes a voice over the studio's PA, "we got this bit before. Let's skip ahead, let's take it from memories and hopes."

"Memories and hopes?" says Dr. Laird, momentarily perplexed. "Memories and hopes? Oh, of course. Right." He closes his eyes for a moment, recalibrating the fine instrument of his soul. "What I'm saying," he finally says, "what I'm saying is that you have nothing but this, nothing but the here and now. I go into this at greater length in *The Wisdom of Wealth*, by the way, for those of you who want to take it further. As I say, nothing but the here, the now. What else have you got? You've got nothing. No past, no future. You've got memories, you've got hopes, yes—but only in the present! Don't you see? This moment is all you've got! Live it now! Live it as though it's your last!"

The first bullet smacks Dr. Laird in the left shoulder, spinning him clockwise, twice. He wobbles briefly before tipping onto his side—an exhausted top. Two more bullets thwack into his prostrate form. After an instant of stunned silence—a moment of presence in the purest sense—people leap to their feet, start scrabbling and clawing their way towards the exits. I allow myself to be carried along with them. I walk a dozen blocks or so—breathing deep, really drinking in the air—and turn down an alleyway. I ditch the gun in one dumpster, my gloves in another.

It's not that he deserved it, that's not what it's about. Tanya would have left me anyway, I understand that, I acknowledge that. If it hadn't been Laird it would have been some other smarmy son of a bitch. No, it's not what you deserve—she explained it to me time and again—it's what you're ready for.

seA peeks

T

"And the master bedroom," says Gail. She stands with her back to the bed, spreads her arms. Her blouse bunches up beneath her breasts, exposes a pale slit of belly.

"Beautiful," says Bill.

"East and west exposure," says Gail. "Very exceptional. And skylights of course." Bill follows her gaze up into the white-blotched azure—he thinks of baby vomit on his good blue shirt. A single gull drifts by overhead. "And from just here," she says, "you've got sea peeks." Bill peers through the western window, between the roofs of neighbouring houses, and believes he has discerned a wedge of choppy Pacific. If so, it's a dream come true.

"And this, *this* will impress your wife," says Gail. She opens a set of louvered doors and steps into an enormous cupboard, running a critical eye over layered racks of clothing. Bill briefly imagines her selecting an outfit—tight tan suede skirt, sleeveless cyan top—and holding it up for his approval.

"Perfect," he says.

It's Monday. Pam and the baby fly in for the weekend on Friday. By then Bill plans to have created a short list, two or three top contenders. Gail has already guided him through countless kitchens, countless bathrooms, countless bedrooms. Together they've laughed at putrid colour schemes, bizarre bits of interior design. Together they've frowned at suspicious cracks in ceilings, poor water pressure. They've snickered like co-conspirators, squabbled like spouses.

"So handy to the bus," Bill will say.

"Yeah, it'll be rumbling by at dawn," Gail will counter.

Over the past couple of weeks, since the company okayed Bill's transfer, he and Gail have settled into a steady routine. Gail picks him up at his hotel after work in her neat little Subaru, does the tour guide thing for him as they zig and zag through town. "Great Italian," she'll say as they pass a vine-hung restaurant, or "Great park for young kids," though he's discovered she's single and childless. They'll do two houses, maybe three, then huddle side by side in her front seat, comparing notes, sharing insights—envisioning for Bill his various futures. Back in his room Bill will place the call. What with the time difference, Pam will be just about ready for bed. She'll hold the phone up to the crib for a while, allow Bill to listen in on the baby's breathing. She'll report on matters digestive, describe in fond detail the colour and consistency of the latest diaper-load. Bill will tell her he loves her, hang up, and call room service for a Reuben sandwich. He'll watch one movie and part of another before falling asleep on top of the covers, still fully clothed. In his dreams Gail will point out to him the outstanding features of certain sexual positions. "What a view!" she'll say. Bill will wake up in the midst of calculating the cost.

Gail says, "This would make a superb nursery, don't you think?" She's led him into another bedroom now, a dim cell redolent of teenage testosterone. The walls are hung with posters of sweaty black men shooting baskets, white women with wet T-shirts—nipples never tugged by a baby's lips. Bill recalls a poster he had over his own bed as a boy, a bikinied bad-girl from a Bond flick crawling up a beach on all fours. And another, a gull swooping low over whitecapped waves, curved wings silhouetted against a sinking sun. Pure getaway, pure flight.

"I think I'd better go home now," says Gail. She's just untangled herself from Bill's embrace. She's tucking in her blouse, running a hand through her hair.

"Home?" says Bill.

raising the sparkS

On the first anniversary of my father's death I began organizing a retrospective of his work focusing on the so-called Postcard Prints, the series of tiny linocuts he produced in his final decade. The result, on the second anniversary of his death, is this exhibition. My intent in these brief curatorial notes is to dispel some of the extraneous mystery surrounding the work, but to leave the central mystery intact.

I've always felt deeply drawn to the pieces in the Postcard series, their concentrated luminosity, the delicate balance they maintain between abstract formality and hints of figurative design. (Besides, my father made a gift to me of one of them near the end of his life, an unwonted show of tenderness.) Many critics, predictably enough, have construed my father's shift to this condensed format—each piece a mere one foot square—as a diminution, an attenuation. His miniatures signify a loss of vitality, they argue, a retreat from his original grand ambitions. Perhaps. Personally, though, I attribute the shift to a refining of his sensibilities, particularly in light of his extensive studies in the East under the masters of *haiga*, that visual equivalent of the delicate, seventeen-syllabled *haiku*. Certainly my father continued to be a willful man, a powerful man: these palm-sized offerings strike me as a conscious rejection of power, a refusal to dictate terms, to overwhelm. They eschew pronouncement in favour of inkling, of implication. As visible fragments they express an acquiescence in his own finite, fragmentary nature.

By the time of my father's death many of the Postcards had already found their way into private collections. It took me some time to track down all hundred and sixty-three and create a master list. It was while poring over this list that I made the discovery responsible for this recent furor.

The first page of titles—compiled in reverse chronological order, most recent to most remote—read as follows:

Olam Ha'Atzilut
Tzimtzum
Tiferet
Netzach
Ein Sof
Ruach
Rachamim
Olam Ha'Asiyah
Hokmah
Binah
Adam Kadmon

It had already been observed that the source of titles for the entire series was the Judaic Kabbalah. There had been much hullabaloo about my father's theology: certain critics imagined him pursuing bizarre occult practices as part of some global cabal, while others branded him a cynic eager to cash in on the current spiritual craze. He was derided too, of course, for cultural appropriation: he was born a German, and no Jew. On the other hand, at least one doctoral thesis had Dad a bona fide seer, the Postcards precise visionary expressions of Kabbalistic concepts. The deepening shades of *Rachamim*, for example, were an embodiment of Compassion; the baroque, almost contrapuntal intricacy of *Adam Kadmon* was my father's rendering of the Body of God.

On all these matters my father maintained his usual magisterial silence. For myself, I doubt Dad even knew the meaning of most of the words. He liked the sound of them—their exoticism, their musical opacity. He liked the fact that they'd make us wonder. And of course he planted them as clues to a larger pattern which none of us, until now, have even suspected.

I've always been a word person, much more so than my father. (Did he bear this in mind as he buried his message? Did he see my discovery all along as part of the bigger picture?) It was second nature for me to discern, as perhaps you have done, the phrase "abhorrent to"—formed by the first letter of each title—running up the left-hand side of that first page. I flipped to the last page of the list, began reading backwards. In chronological order, the titles of the Postcard series turn out to constitute the following acronym (I've added spaces and punctuation):

> *A raindrop absorbed by the sea is, after all, no raindrop. As fragments we take pleasure only in fragments, must expend our lives in ever more elaborate evasions of the totality which is so abhorrent to . . .*

I've experienced a few moments of revelation in my four decades of life. There was the day I found out that my mother wasn't my mother (or rather, that she had adopted rather than given birth to me); there was the day I discovered that my father hadn't died (as my birth mother claimed for so many years after

I found her), but had simply chosen his muse over my mother and me. This new revelation was on a par with those others. Space and time shifted, split open: my father was a conundrum to me once again.

If my father had conceived the titles of the whole series at one sitting, to generate this abstruse code for us, then it seemed likely the pieces themselves had been created according to some master scheme as well—that they were interconnected in some way we hadn't yet recognized. Perhaps you can imagine the fervour, the febrile anticipation with which I set about gathering the works and laying them side by side, looking for links, patterns. After several days of trial and error I stumbled on the puzzle's key. The pieces do indeed combine to form one large image, eleven feet by fifteen. Chronologically, in order of composition, they first outline the perimeter and then gradually spiral in towards the centre. At the bull's eye there is, as you will see, a two-foot void. My father succumbed before he could finish "us."

"A raindrop absorbed by the sea . . ." What was he driving at? What was the source of this dark fragment? Two months prior to his passing away my father cited the text for us. He granted an interview—rare, almost unheard of—in which he quoted the lines and attributed them to Otto Rank, one of Freud's wayward disciples. Rehabilitating Rank—who saw the neurotic as the *artiste-manqué*, the artist bereft of calling—was a pet project of my father's. There's a hefty Rank section in the library he left behind. Nowhere in that library—or in any of Rank's works, as far as I can tell—are those lines to be found. Ornery old man.

"Abhorrent to us?" wondered the interviewer. "Why would totality be abhorrent to us?"

"Because," my father explained, "totality, or wholeness, signifies union. Union signifies death—the object of our most profound ambivalence, our deepest desire and disgust."

My father never used the word *tikkun* as one of his titles, but he knew of it, and highlighted it in the single book on Kabbalah we find in his collection. I suspect it was this concept that drew him to Kabbalah in the first place, as a source of esoteric-sounding words. *Tikkun* refers to the "raising of the sparks," the piecing back together of the original light which was shattered in creation, in the act of withdrawal through which the Absolute gave birth to existence. The Postcard Series, as I conceive it now, is an expression of my father's own ambivalence about wholeness, the love/hate relationship he had with completion. I can't entirely discount my birth mother's claim that the wholeness my father desired and dreaded was that of his own family (though I may question her motivation in going public at a time when my father's stock is so dramatically on the rise). Similarly, the near-figurative design which dominates the assembled Postcards may be a pity, a *pietà*, mother and son. And then again, it may not.

T

the End of the world

"Have you been on one before?" I said. "A blind date, I mean?" Like it was any of my business—I'd known the woman about forty-five minutes, most of it spent driving around in my minivan looking for a parking spot within a high-heeled walk of the Pensive Flamingo. It was the last pub I'd visited, and that three years earlier. I was stunned to find it standing.

"Once," said Pamina—I'd already scored a couple of points for twigging to this name from *The Magic Flute*. Her dad had been a Mozart man. "About a year ago, which was about a year after my husband— Oh, um, just a Perrier."

"Same for me," I said. I'd have paid big bucks for a margarita. "You were saying?"

"Yes, my one blind date," she said. "My mother talked me into it. He was the son of a friend of a friend of hers. A mathematician, very smart."

"Did you see him again?"

"No."

Pause. "I've been on one other as well," I volunteered. "My kids pressured me into it. Sick of feeling sorry for me."

A rueful smile, no laugh. She ran a hand through her hennaed hair, exposing a few grey roots.

"It's crazy," I said, for no particular reason. I was trying not to look at her breasts, or rather to look *for* her breasts. I'd always wondered what it would be like to be with a really flat-chested woman. The idea excited me—some sort of homoerotic rush, I suppose.

"He said one kind of interesting thing," said Pamina. "My blind date. We were at my place having a drink before we went out. I can't remember what I said, and then he said, '*Eternity is in love with the productions of time.*' Or something like that. I said to him, 'That sounds like a quote,' and he said, 'Yeah, but then again, almost anything anybody ever says is a quote.' Thanks."

The waiter set down our drinks. We sipped, adjusted our cocktail napkins. Should have risked a beer. How did this other oaf rate a drink at her place?

"Then he started talking mathematics," she went on. "He started talking about the probability that what anybody's saying at any given moment is actually a quote, whether they know it or not. The probability that any words, these words, for instance, have been said before. The longer the world drags on—I think he actually said that, 'the longer the world *drags on*'—the higher that probability becomes. In other words, the less likely it is you're saying anything even remotely original."

"Really," I said.

"Really. He was trying to work out whether or not there'll be an end to all this." She made a sweeping gesture with her left, non-Perrier hand, indicating our surroundings, the dim, bluish bar with its little clusters of chatting people. "Whether there'll come a time when there's literally nothing left to say. Mathematically speaking. 'The end of the world,' is how he put it."

"Oh, I don't think so," I said. I hadn't touched a woman in over a year, you understand, since well before Molly finally left. "No, I don't think so at all. I think nothing has ever been said more than once. I mean, even if I quote somebody, and I know I'm quoting them, I won't really be quoting them. I won't be saying the same thing they said. I could say to you, '*We know the story is complete when the worst possible thing happens*'—I could say that, and know I'm quoting, but I wouldn't be quoting. I wouldn't be saying the same thing as the guy who said it. God you're beautiful."

"Funny," she could have said, "that's what he said." This would have been the worst possible thing. But she said something else, and then I said something, and then she said, "Catch the waiter, would you? I feel like something a little stronger," and, "*Pamina*," I suddenly crooned, phony opera voice, "*Pamina, sie . . . lebt*, is it? Lives?" and this was just the beginning.

new stoRy

He presses his forehead against the bathroom door. "Helen?" he says. "Helen, how long are you going to be in there?"

From behind the door, the sound of sloshing water.

"Honey, you'll turn into a prune," he says.

Silence.

"Helen, talk to me."

"No!" Her voice reaches him as a muffled echo, as though from some deep dank cavern.

"Thank you," he says. "Now, tell me. What did I say?"

"You didn't say anything," she says.

"Pardon, honey, I can't quite—"

"You didn't say anything."

"What did I do then?" He places his palms on the top of the door frame, flexes his arms and shoulders as though testing the weight of the roof.

"We used to live in the water," she says. "Did you know that?"

"Just a little louder, sweetheart."

"We used to live in the water. For ten million years we lived in the water, in the ocean, by the shore. That's why we got up on our hind legs in the first place, to keep our heads above the surface."

"Was it something I did tonight?" he says. "When Jennifer and Tom were here? Just tell me."

"There was this big drought and we had to come down out of the trees," she says. "In the old story we moved onto the plains so the men could hunt. This is the new story."

"Was it something I did before work this morning? Was it that thing with the cat? Come on, be fair." On cue the cat, Tet—short for Bastet, after the divine Egyptian puss—pads out of the bedroom, executes a couple of brisk figure eights around his shins, and trots mrowing down the stairs.

"In the new story," she says, "we slipped into the ocean and became fishers."

"Became what, honey?"

"Became *fishers.* Fishers. All of us, men and women. Our first tools weren't for cracking skulls, they were for cracking shells. Like sea otters do. We lost our fur and started putting on fat, like hippopotamuses."

"Hippopotami," he says. "I think that's hippopotami, honey. But was it something I did on the weekend? At my parents' place maybe?"

"We weren't chasing anything, we were escaping, we were *getting away* from all the things that wanted to harm us."

"Helen, this is ridiculous," he says. "Can I just come in? Let me come in."

"We grew long hair on our heads for our babies to hang onto. Our babies grew fat and buoyant, we grew big buoyant breasts for them to cling to while they suckled."

He says, "I'm coming in, okay? Helen?"

"And when we cried, we cried salty tears. Only sea creatures cry salty tears, did you know that?"

“Here I come,” he says, and he opens the door.

It’s a big clawfoot tub, painted deep blue but chipped here and there to reveal little islands of white. She’s stretched out almost full length. Her breasts bob above the water, as does the startling swell of her belly, taut, tawny. Her long dark hair is spread like kelp across the surface.

“Why did we get out?” she says. She presses each of her eyes with the heel of one hand, licks it. “Why would we ever get out?”

“It was that thing about your mother last week, wasn’t it?” he says. But he has the feeling he’s going to have to go back even further.

Acknowledgements

Thanks to the British Columbia Arts Council for financial assistance during the writing of this book. Thanks to friends and family for their inspiration and support, especially to Sandy Mayzell, George and Joan Anne Gould, Jane Fairbanks, Alex Stein, and the members of my wonderful writing community: Patricia Young, Terence Young, and so many others. Thanks to Jonathan and Amanda Chesley for smartening me up. Special thanks to the most attentive reader of all, my sister, Anne Louise Gould, who has lovingly deciphered me since day one. For their acuity and enthusiasm, thanks finally to my agent, Kathryn Mulders, to my editor, Wayne Tefs, and to Todd Besant and all at Turnstone Press.

A number of quotations from other works appear in several stories in my collection.

In "Leather," the phrase "More I would, but death invades me," is from Henry Purcell's *Dido and Aeneas.*

"I will make him an help meet for him," in "Feelers," is from Genesis 2:18.

In "Conversion," the following quotations are from *Pensées* by Blaise Pascal, translated by W.F. Trotter. Section II, Part 71: "Too much and too little wine. Give him none, he cannot find truth; give him too much, the same." Section VII, Part 553: "Jesus will be in agony even to the end of the world. We must not sleep during that time."

Several lines from the traditional gospel song "Swing Low, Sweet Chariot" are used throughout the story "Sweet Chariot."

In "Takeout," the excerpt, "At last the bottom fell out. No more water in the pail. No more moon in the water," is from *Zen Flesh Zen Bones* by Paul Reps, published by Charles E. Tuttle Co., Inc. (Boston, Massachusetts and Tokyo, Japan), used by permission.

The excerpts from the pamphlet *Nine things you will know when you are a Bahá'í* quoted in "Conviction" are used by permission of the publishers of www.special-ideas.com.

The William Wordsworth quotation in "Password" is from "Ode: Intimations of Immortality From Recollections of Early Childhood."

"Neither Nor" quotes the Heart Sutra of Buddha. The sentence "Only he knows the divine who recognizes that all creatures are nothingness . . . If the soul is to know the divine it must forget itself and lose itself. . . ." is from Meister Eckhart's sermon "The Nearness of the Kingdom."

"Dust" contains several quotations from *The Book of Job* by Stephen Mitchell, translator, HarperCollins Publishers Inc. (New York), 1979. Used by permission. "If only I had strangled or drowned, on my way down to the bitter light,"; "Silence and peace have abandoned me, and anguish camps in my heart,"; "I will be quiet, comforted that I am dust."

In "Suite," "Misterioso, Misterioso altero, croce, croce e delizia," is from *La Traviata* by Guiseppe Verdi.

The John Donne quotation in "The Point of Dreaming" is from Holy Sonnet 10.

"The End of the Day" opens with a quotation from *The Wonderful Wizard of Oz* by Frank Baum.

"All Mysteries" contains a quotation from I Corinthians 13, the King James Bible.

In "The End of the World," the sentence "Eternity is in love with the productions of time," is from *The Marriage of Heaven and Hell* by William Blake. "Pamina, Pamina sie . . . lebt. . . ." is from *The Magic Flute* by Wolfgang Amadeus Mozart.